MILES LEDOUX

THE THIRD WILL

Winter in Veil, Book 8

Prologue

Cy stood at the top of the pearl-white hill, the slopes glittering with fresh snow. She inhaled deeply through her nose, relishing the scent of winter. It was surprising that there was no one else here; a clear day like today, the conditions were perfect for sledding.

As if on cue, a shadow appeared on the ground next to her. Someone was approaching from behind. She turned. "Luther!" she exclaimed with a smile.

"Hey," said Luther, displaying his signature bashful grin. He gave her an awkward one-armed hug. They'd started dating a few weeks ago. Given the direction her previous relationship had gone, Cy was taking it slow.

"What are you doing here?" asked Cy.

"I was out for a walk. I saw you standing here—though I wasn't sure it was you." He tugged playfully at her form-obscuring winter jacket.

Cy pulled back her hood and looked out over the hill. "Do you ever come sledding here?"

"I'm more of a skier."

"Right. You told me." Cy sighed gently. "My dad used to take me sledding here. When my grandfather still lived in Veil, we'd come visit him on winter vacation. Dad and I always came to this hill at least once. It was our thing." Her chin drooped. She

1

felt Luther put his hand on her shoulder in sympathy. It gave her a warm feeling. Leaning against him, she said, "With the way things are now between him and me, I'm not sure how to feel about this place. I guess I came here to try to…" She trailed off, a frown appearing on her face. "Wait a second." She pulled away from Luther, pivoting to face him. "I thought you said you weren't going to be back from vacation until the day before school starts again."

Luther shifted uncomfortably. "W-well…" Before he could get any farther, his foot slipped on an icy patch of snow, and all at once he was sliding down the hillside, limbs flailing.

"Luther!" Cy tried to run after him, but within moments she, too, was sliding down, out of control and picking up speed. She tried to orient herself so she could see Luther, but it was no use. The landscape spun around her faster and faster, it was making her queasy. She shut her eyes to make it stop, but it only seemed to make the feeling worse. She opened her eyes—

—and found herself in a dimly lit room, lying on her back, on the floor. She'd been dreaming.

Her first impulse was to sit up quickly, but her lingering queasiness and the dull ache in her skull told her that would be a bad idea. Where was she? The room's only light source was a small window high up on the wall. Two of the walls were lined with shelves, but from down here, she couldn't make out what was on them. There was a cupboard in the corner. The floor beneath her was hard… Concrete?

How did she get here? What day was it? Her best friend, Violet, had a perfect memory. Such a gift would come in handy in a situation like this.

Violet—her friend's name sparked a sense of urgency. Something about Violet… Something Cy had to do…to help her…

Wincing, fighting dizziness, Cy slowly pushed herself to her feet. Her surroundings swam into focus. Most of the shelves were bare, but a few held pairs of boots. No, not boots—skates! Ice skates. Interspersed between them were a few crumpled hockey jerseys. Part of a helmet was visible on the floor of the open cupboard. In the corner of the room lay a heap of championship banners of varying colors.

She must be at the Greene River Ice Rink—in a storage closet, no less (one they didn't use anymore, it looked like). But how did she get here? The ice rink was two towns away! She couldn't remember leaving Veil—

Wait. That wasn't right—she *had* left Veil, but only as far as Platte…

Suddenly, Cy knew exactly where she was, and it was somewhere she shouldn't be. Wheeling about, she shot toward the door and turned the handle. She felt the catch release, but the door wouldn't budge. Something was blocking it on the other side. Frantically, Cy kicked and heaved at the door, for it was all coming back to her—Violet—Roberta Lammwych—the online alert—the ghost…

Faintly Cy heard a noise from beyond the door. Instantly she froze, straining her ears. She couldn't hear anything apart from her own rapid breathing, but deep in her gut she was certain she wasn't alone.

Out of habit, she reached into her pocket, knowing she wouldn't find anything there. Whoever had knocked her out and put her here wouldn't have risked leaving her with her cell phone.

To her surprise, her phone was still there.

Cy whipped out the phone and called her mother, who also happened to be a deputy with the sheriff's department.

"Cy?!"

"Mom!" Cy whispered. "I need your help!"

"Where are you?"

"I'm locked in a storage closet! I think I'm at the—" Cy's heart doubled over at the sound of approaching footsteps. She fought to keep her jaw from trembling, her voice from squeaking. "Mom, someone's coming! I'm scared!"

"Cy, listen!" It was a new voice.

"Violet??"

"Cy, listen to me! Go to the corner of the room."

"What??"

"The corner of the room, where the banners are."

"How do you know about—"

"I'll explain later, just hurry!"

The footsteps neared the door. There was a heavy, crunching sound. Whatever had been blocking the door, it was being moved aside.

Cy shrank against the banners in the corner. "They're coming in!"

"Cy, listen—behind the banners—" Abruptly her voice distorted and grew silent.

"Violet? Violet!"

The heavy object went silent. The door was unblocked. Whoever was there was about to enter.

Cy threw aside the banners—and discovered the square entrance to a vent!

The doorknob turned.

Cy dove into the vent and crawled as fast as she could. It was almost pitch dark. When the crawlspace bent sharply to the left, Cy nearly ran headlong into the vent wall.

"Cy! Cy, can you hear me?"

4

"Violet!" The call hadn't dropped after all. Cy tried not to bump her head as she held the phone to her ear and crawled at the same time.

"Are you in the vent?"

"Yes," she whispered.

"Are they following you?"

Cy halted, tried to quiet her breathing. There didn't seem to be any noise behind her. "I don't think so."

"Okay, have you gotten to where the vent turns to the left?"

"Y-yeah. Violet, how do you—"

"After another few feet, you'll come to a T-intersection. Go right."

Cy crawled on and found that it was just as Violet said. She turned right.

"Next you're going to come to a spot where you can turn left or go straight. Go straight."

"Okay." Under the circumstances, Cy was more than happy to wait until Violet had guided her all the way to safety before pressing her as to how she was so familiar with the vent network.

However, when she reached the next juncture Violet had described, she faltered. The passage ahead had a lower ceiling, leaving barely enough room even for a slim person like Cy. She slithered into it like a worm, but once inside, crawling was much more difficult. She found her breath coming faster, louder, her heart racing.

"Cy? Cy!"

"I can't do this!"

"Cy, listen to me. Pause and take a breath."

"It's too small! I can't move!"

"Cy—breathe and listen to me. You will get through this, I promise. I'm going to guide you."

"I want my mom!"

"She just went into the vents."

"Wh-what?"

"We're all outside—me, the sheriff, the deputies—we're standing where the vent comes out, but Jen went in from this end to meet you. You're not alone, Cy."

Cy's breath quieted. "Okay."

Cy put her phone on speaker and stuffed it down the front of her jacket. Crawl by crawl, meter by meter, with Violet's guidance, she navigated the vents. Here and there she glimpsed light from adjacent tunnels, but Violet advised her to stick to the route she had plotted. Cy trusted her friend's judgment.

Hours later, or so it seemed, as Cy's elbows and hips groaned in protest, Violet's voice suddenly took on a tone of excitement. *"You're almost there, Cy!"* she reassured her. *"And when you turn left at the next T, you should see your mom."*

Ignoring the complaints of her joints, Cy sped up. She turned the next corner so fast, she rolled herself over onto her side. "I see her!" she cried in delight. "Mom, I'm here!"

The figure several meters away immediately began approaching more rapidly. A bright light dazzled Cy's eyes. The girl put up a hand. "Aagh, Mom, I'm not going anywhere. Quit shining the light in my face."

But the light stayed pointed right in her eyes.

"Cy...get out of there."

"What?"

"Get out of there!"

"But—Mom is—"

"Your mother doesn't have a flashlight!!"

The figure behind the light closed in even faster.

With a shriek of terror, Cy backtracked along the tunnel—

turning around was impossible. Her knees were battered and bruised, but she didn't stop—her pursuer was moving faster than she was. She could hear them breathing—low, guttural, bestial...

She made it back to the last intersection. She backed into one avenue, then changed direction and faced forward again. Now she could speed up—

Cy felt a powerful hand close around her ankle. She screamed...

I

TWENTY-FOUR HOURS EARLIER...

Dear Azura,
　　It's cool of you to give me a reason to practice my typing—I'm getting better at writing essays and letters on the computer without the keyboard giving me a stress attack—but seriously, you guys have got to get your phones fixed down there. Even I'm worried about you.

Let's see, news headlines from Veil...

Myrna Redpath got her power back yesterday, so we're finally all recovered from the ice storm. Well, that's not completely true, some people are still displaced because their homes were damaged. I liked having the Dosleys over, it gave me and Kristy a chance to get to know each other better. I think Roswell bonded with the baby.

Kurt Riner was transferred to the county jail yesterday. I think everyone's relieved he's finally gone from the town, waiting for his trial. Apparently he's still swearing he's innocent. Violet is convinced he's guilty, so I'm not letting it worry me. I trust her.

I think Violet's finally starting to like living here in Veil. She hasn't given up trying to find out her true identity, but she's let *herself become part of the community. I guess so have I. I've even decorated my bedroom—finally.*

Em and Neesha still aren't talking to me, but I've started to make other friends. Luther says he wishes he was less shy so he could introduce me to his friends, if he had any. When school starts up again, I'm going to volunteer for the school paper. Wish me luck.

That's about it for now. I'd tell you about the weather, but you've probably got enough snow of your own down in Antarctica that you're sick of hearing about it.

I miss you. I can't wait till you come home in May and I can introduce you to Violet and Luther—assuming we're still dating then.

Stay warm, Booger.

- Cy

* * *

Violet spun about with a gasp. It was the third time she'd done so today. Just as with the previous two occasions, there was no one lurking behind her. Why did she keep having that feeling?

She drew a deep breath, inhaling the flavorful aroma of exotic herbs and spices, and tried to rein in her focus back to the present. One by one, she pressed the tip of the label gun to the jars of blackberry jam sitting on the shelf.

Between the mystery of her own identity and the startling frequency of crime in this small town, Violet's interests had tended toward a career as an investigator, perhaps a sheriff's deputy. Nevertheless, while she pursued her goals, she needed to earn a living. On this she'd insisted, regardless of her hosts' ongoing generosity.

Two months ago, she'd helped prevent the abduction of a baby girl. The baby's thirty-nine-year-old grandmother showed her gratitude by giving Violet a part-time job in her dry goods store on Main Street, *'Tis the Seasoning*—an interesting name, Violet thought, given that the grandmother and her family were Jewish.

The best thing about working here, Violet had found, was that it gave her a chance to truly become acquainted with the Veil townsfolk. Among the store's patrons, she met Trevor Burns, a professional snow plower (and lawn mower in the summer) who was also a stage magician. She met Eva MacNeil, a sex ed teacher who had once been a pole dancer. With the gift of a perfect memory, Violet could have retained the surface details even if they'd been mentioned in passing amidst a flurry of other trivia, but she preferred it like this. Getting to speak to people one at a time, in a quiet little shop where the pace was slow, suited her much better. She was able to get to know her neighbors for who they were, rather than just sets of memorized facts.

"Violet?" called the diminutive Joy Dosley from the register. "Would you help this gentleman while I take a delivery?"

"Yeah, sure!" Violet laid the label gun on a shelf and headed for the register. The man standing there was someone she'd never seen before. He was tall, thin, in his forties, she guessed. Depending on how talkative he was, she might be about to make a new friend.

"How can I help you?" she asked from behind the register. The man hadn't brought any items to the counter, so he probably wanted to ask a question.

"You're Violet?" The man had a pleasant, if a bit oily, voice. It went with the suit and tie poking out from the collar of his heavy winter coat.

"That's me," said Violet. Occasionally people came to the store just to satisfy their curiosity about her. It had been awkward at first, but with Cy's help she'd reached the point where she didn't mind anymore.

The man reached into a pocket, withdrew an envelope, and held it out to her. "You've been served."

Violet blinked. "Excuse me?"

Since she hadn't taken the proffered envelope, the man laid it on the counter. "My name is Henry Glass. My clients are suing you for identity fraud."

Violet came close to laughing, but the lawyer's steady gaze extinguished the impulse. His eyes betrayed a hint of smugness. "I think you're mistaking me for someone else," she told him.

Glass smiled and shook his head. "No," he said. Then he turned to leave.

"Wait a minute!" Violet ran out in front of him. "I don't know anything about this! I haven't—I haven't claimed a false identity! I've spent the last three months trying to find *out* my identity!"

"How very philosophical," Glass said with amused disinterest.

"Who is it I'm supposed to have claimed to be?" Violet demanded. "And when?"

Glass drew a breath with an affected air of patience. "I have found ample evidence that on October fifteenth of last year, you made claim to the identity of Roberta Lammwych."

Violet's head reeled. Lammwych was a name she'd run into on several occasions here in Veil. But the very first time she'd heard it—October fifteenth—was a day that burned glaringly bright in her memory, for it was the earliest day she could remember. It was the day she'd woken up with amnesia.

Cy was the first person she'd encountered, and Violet still couldn't believe her luck. Operating on the theory that someone in Veil must know her true identity, Cy had kindly taken Violet under her wing and tried to help her find that someone. One of the first people they'd consulted was Delphine Burgess, an elderly woman who knew practically everyone in Veil. Delphine had indeed recognized Violet—or thought she did.

Violet gave Glass a very strange look. "You don't mean the Roberta Lammwych who disappeared *forty-two years ago?*"

"The very same."

This time Violet did laugh. "You've definitely gotten your facts mixed up. I've never claimed to be that woman. Someone once…" She paused, remembering Delphine overcome with excitement, certain that she was in the presence of the vanished Roberta, convinced that Violet was the reincarnation of the woman's spirit. It had taken much coaxing by bystanders to persuade Delphine that such was not the case. "Someone once *suggested* that I'm Roberta, but no one took it seriously— certainly not me."

Glass took a nonchalant step toward her, his shoes echoing on the wood-paneled floor. "You say someone 'suggested' it."

"That's right."

Glass took another step, laid his fingers on a container of sage, as if distracted. "Did they suggest it…as a joke?"

"N-no, not exactly."

"Hm." Glass turned his attention to a sprig of lavender. "Of course this person's 'suggestion' wasn't in any way…prompted by you, was it?"

"What? No, of course not!"

"I see. So this alleged person just randomly and arbitrarily 'suggested' that you were Roberta Lammwych, an individual who, when located, just happens to be in line to inherit a substantial fortune."

Taken aback, Violet struggled to maintain her focus. "I didn't ask at the time why she said it, but until that moment, *I had never heard of Roberta Lammwych.*"

"So naturally you refuted the suggestion."

Whatever Violet might have been about to say died on the tip of her tongue. She recalled her desperation on that first day, her urgency, her overwhelming need to find out who she really was. Delphine had gotten Violet's hopes up at first, identifying her as the missing woman, but when it later came out that the woman had vanished almost half a century ago, Violet had walked away in a huff, lest she flip out in front of all those strangers.

"I had other things on my mind!" she protested. Then, suddenly wondering why she was on the defensive, she added, "Besides, there wasn't any *need* to refute it! It was an absurd idea! I'm clearly not old enough to be Roberta! No one would believe it!"

"And yet someone suggested it—without any prompt from you, or so you said." At last, he looked her in the eye. She could see the gleam of triumph that she'd fallen into his trap.

Shaking her head in disgust, she grabbed the envelope from the counter and held it out to him. "Look, this is ridiculous. Just tell your clients I'm not after their money—or Roberta's, or whatever. If they want me to sign something swearing I'm not Roberta Lammwych, I'll do it. There's no need for a lawsuit."

For a moment Glass didn't move or speak. Then he reached out slowly, as if with deliberate consideration, and started to grasp the envelope. Violet had just begun to breathe a sigh of relief when he said, "So you're retracting your insinuation that you're Roberta Lammwych?"

Violet might have been short, but she could still level a decimating glare, and glare she did. "I can't retract a statement that I never made to begin with."

With an exaggerated expression of regret, Glass let go of the envelope. "I'm afraid that's not going to be good enough for my clients."

Violet stared at him incredulously. "If your clients are so worried about me, why did they wait so long? Why didn't they just come to me? We could've talked and worked it out—"

"An attempt was made to contact you over a month ago."

This brought her up short. "How?"

"Correspondence was mailed to you, care of the Veil Sheriff's Department."

"I never got it!!"

Glass shrugged with a sorrowful smile—though Violet could tell he wasn't sorry at all. "Then my clients are going to have to take you to court." He strode to the door, then pivoted back and, after a measured pause, said, "I doubt that a courthouse is the most optimal place for a person...with no identity."

Snow billowed through the door as he exited.

* * *

"Found it!" cried Deputy Hayden, brandishing a white envelope as she burst into the sheriff's office.

Violet, Deputy Jen Grogan, and Sheriff Dubowski gathered around the desk as Hayden set down the envelope. It was addressed *To the woman representing herself as Roberta Lammwych.*

"I remember now," said the sheriff. "None of us knew what it was talking about, and we were all still dealing with the aftermath of the serial killer, and..." He trailed off. Violet knew he was thinking of Kurt Riner, his best friend, whom she had unmasked as the killer. The sheriff hadn't been himself since. "When the ice storm hit," he went on, "we filed it and forgot about it." He patted Hayden absently on the shoulder. "Glad someone remembered."

Hayden blushed.

Violet forcefully tore open the envelope, eliciting a raised eyebrow from Jen. When the senior deputy first took her into her home, Violet had been timid and, all in all, meek. The serial killer crisis seemed to have brought out her more assertive side. She might not make a bad deputy someday after all.

Violet unfolded the letter and laid it flat for all to see. It was exactly as Glass had said, a cease-and-desist message directed at her. *Your inability to provide valid identification will not indemnify you from prosecution,* it said, among other things. But Violet's attention was drawn to the date. She laid her finger on it. "November nineteenth."

Dubowski nodded. "Over a month ago, just like the lawyer said."

"No, I mean…that was the day after we caught—the serial killer."

Jen frowned. "Is that significant?"

"I feel like it is," Violet said after a moment.

Reading through the letter, Jen made a noise of disgust. "This is insane. Violet doesn't really have to take this seriously, does she?"

The sheriff grimaced. "I'm not sure," he sighed. "I'm not a lawyer."

"Are there any in Veil?" asked Violet.

A troubled look passed over the sheriff's face. "Kurt was a prosecutor, but unofficially he was Veil's go-to person for legal advice. The only other person in town with legal experience would've been…"

"Amy," Jen finished quietly. Amy Chester had been one of the serial killer's victims. She and Jen had a complicated history.

Violet deflated. "What am I supposed to do now?"

15

No one answered.

The phone on the desk rang. The sheriff picked it up. "Dubowski."

Violet's eyes narrowed. She picked up the envelope and squinted at the return address in the upper left corner. Then she pulled out the envelope she'd received earlier and did the same.

"What is it?" asked Jen.

"The return addresses are different." Violet showed her each envelope in turn. "The one he gave me in person is from his firm in Brattleboro. But this one came from an address in Platte. Isn't that the hamlet just outside Veil? The one some people call Veil's suburb?"

"It is, but don't let anyone in Platte hear you say that."

Violet looked at the clock. It was almost two in the afternoon. "If I could talk to these people, maybe I could convince them they don't need to sue me."

Jen nodded slowly. "It's possible."

The sheriff hung up with a grim expression.

Violet made a show of cringing away from Jen. "Would you… go with me?"

Jen gave her a severe scowl, but it lasted only a few seconds before it broke into a grin. "Of course I will."

"I'm afraid she can't," said the sheriff. "Grogan, I need you and Benno with me. We, um… There's been a mysterious death."

Both Jen and Violet felt goosebumps rise on their skin. Veil had had more than its share of deaths over the past few months. Things had only gone from bad to worse up until the night the serial killer was caught. There weren't supposed to be any more "mysterious" deaths. Veil had suffered enough.

"Is it—homicide?" asked Deputy Hayden.

16

The sheriff took his jacket from a hook on the wall, turned back to his deputies, opened his mouth to speak, but then hesitated. "Let's go," he finally said, leading the way out.

II

P latte, Vermont, gave new meaning to the phrase, "Blink and you'll miss it." Almost a mile from Veil, it consisted of a gas station, a small restaurant, and a smattering of houses and barns, all dispersed about a single intersection. An old, rusty sign pointed the way toward the Platte Ice Rink, but a newer sign covered it, reading, *CLOSED*.

If Violet had been under the impression that frivolous lawsuits were made only by the rich, the sight of the Lammwych family home quickly disabused her. She and Cy dismounted their bicycles and leaned them against a tree, gazing up at the large house, much of which was in disrepair. The garage sitting next to it had completely fallen apart. Two pickup trucks were parked in front of it.

Making an effort not to dwell on what she'd just heard at the sheriff's station—and the possibility of yet another murderer in Veil—Violet strode toward the front door covered in chipping white paint.

"I still think you should hire your own lawyer," Cy remarked.

"Apparently the only two lawyers in Veil were Kurt and Amy."

"Hm," Cy grunted. "I could be your lawyer."

Violet threw her an amused grin.

"No, seriously. Azura and I were raised on *Matlock* and *Perry Mason*. I could totally represent you."

Violet yelped as she stepped on a broken piece of flagstone under the snow and lost her footing. Cy caught her and kept her from falling. "Thanks," gasped Violet. She kept hold of Cy's arm the rest of the way up the path. "I thought you wanted to be a journalist, not a lawyer."

Cy shrugged. "It's easy to want to be something when you're pissed. Remember the day we met? Being pissed at my ex-boyfriend turned me into a public speaker. The journalist thing was a result of us constantly running into Kelly Upshaw."

Violet's responding grunt more resembled a groan. The reporter from the local paper had, among other things, repeatedly insinuated that Violet was faking her amnesia. Each successive encounter had deepened the mutual dislike between them.

When they reached the door, Violet let go of Cy and rapped three times with the door knocker. Within moments the door was answered by a vacant-looking man in his mid-twenties, wearing a stained hoodie. He stood, slouched, in the doorway without expression, though it seemed, rather than being furtive, he simply had no interest in feeling emotion. He was thin almost to the point of emaciation.

When he didn't say anything, Violet stammered, "Hi. I'm— Violet. I'm here to talk to the Lammwyches."

The man continued to stare vacantly.

"About the lawsuit," Violet clarified, reddening.

For a moment more, he said nothing, then— "URSULA!"

Both Cy and Violet jumped; the man had a surprisingly booming voice. Then, even more surprisingly, he turned away in disinterest and retreated inside the house, leaving the door wide open. Cy and Violet exchanged uncertain glances.

19

A rapid series of heavy footfalls signaled someone's descent of a staircase. With startling abruptness, a tall, slim, fiftyish woman appeared before them. It was hard to tell her expression under all the makeup she wore, but she looked peeved.

Violet felt a sense of familiarity; had she seen this woman before? "Hi," she tried again, "I'm—"

"You're Violet!" the woman exclaimed.

"Yes. I—"

"Boy, you've got a lot of nerve coming here to my door." She stepped over the threshold, looming over Violet and radiating hostility. "What do you want, huh?"

"I—just—thought we could talk—"

"I'm not interested in talking. You can say what you want to say in court." She stepped back inside and made as if to shut the door.

"But—" Violet shook her head in desperation. "I can't go to court! Can't we just—"

"You don't wanna go to court? Fine." The woman leaned out of the doorway. "We won't sue you—if you leave Veil."

Violet stared at her, aghast. "What?!"

"No courtroom if you get out of town. Take it or leave it." The woman started to close the door.

"Excuse me!" Cy stepped forward with a scowl of outrage.

Ursula Lammwych looked at her askance. "Who are you?"

"Cyanne Grogan. I'm Violet's attorney."

Violet winced. Due to their difference in stature, Cy might appear older than Violet, but there was no way anyone could believe she was old enough to hold a law degree.

Cy, nevertheless, plowed on. "My client only first heard of this so-called lawsuit today. She's willing to sort all of this out here and now—"

"I don't want it sorted out. I want her gone." Ursula fixed a predatory eye on Violet, making her draw back.

Cy stepped in front of her. "Well, she's not going anywhere! You want to go to court? We'll go to court. But do you realize, now that you've admitted your suit is intended to be, um, *coercive* rather than *punitive*, and that by denying her the chance to talk with you to settle the matter, you're giving us a strong case that *you're wasting the court's time?* Violet is obviously not Roberta Lammwych. Your case is gonna get thrown out like *that*." She snapped her fingers.

Ursula glared at her with clenched jaw, clearly hovering between spitting a response and slamming the door in their faces.

"Let her in," rumbled a man's deep voice from within the house.

Leaning over, Violet peered past Cy and Ursula, but she couldn't make out the speaker.

Ursula's lip formed an angry pout, but after a moment she stood aside to let them enter.

"Not the lawyer," the voice spoke again. "Just Violet."

Cy turned to Violet, her brow creased with concern. "I'll be all right," Violet assured her. Approaching the threshold, she felt Cy squeeze her hand. Then her nostrils filled with cigarette smoke and perfume. Holding her breath, she stepped through the door and heard it close behind her.

* * *

Jen was plenty warm under her jacket, yet she shivered as she regarded the corpse in front of her.

"Deceased's name is Sharon Brisbon," she heard Deputy Benno report to the sheriff behind her. "Age: eighty-four. Lived in Veil since the late nineteen-nineties."

Jen cast her mind back to the nineties—she would've been in her teens—but she couldn't remember ever knowing this woman existed. Then again, her appearance would likely have been quite different back then.

"Coroner estimates the time of death was approximately 7 a.m. Cause of death…"

"Exposure," murmured the sheriff, stepping to Jen's side. The dead woman lay as if asleep, her skin whiter than Jen had ever thought possible for a human being. The day had already reached its peak of thirty-eight degrees Fahrenheit—warm for this time of year—but the night before, it would've been much, much colder. Yet all the woman wore was a threadbare robe and a pair of faded pink slippers.

"Did the coroner mention how long he thought Ms. Brisbon had been lying here before she expired?" asked Dubowski, evidently following the same train of thought as Jen.

"His guess was about five hours maximum," said Benno. "There are no signs of physical assault or restraint. He figures she just had a moment of absent-mindedness, probably took a sleeping drug that made her so drowsy she didn't notice how cold she was."

"But why come outside at all?" Jen wondered aloud. They were standing on a deck behind the old woman's house. A sliding door led into her living room. The reclining deck chair the woman was lying on was one of five, all padded.

The sheriff shrugged, gazing out at the sparkling countryside. "It's a gorgeous view from here," he remarked. "Last night it was clear, with a full moon. It would've been a beautiful sight. I can imagine her stepping outside to enjoy the view just before bed, losing track of time…"

Jen frowned, casting her eyes over the scene again and again.

In a quieter voice, the sheriff asked, "What's eating you, Jen?"

She looked at him and hesitated.

Keeping his eyes on hers, Dubowski said, "Benno, tell the coroner he can have the body." As Benno headed back through the house, the sheriff and his senior deputy stepped off the deck and into the snowy yard.

"Sheriff," Jen said slowly, "the last couple days, I've had three people ask me if a certain rumor is true."

"What rumor?"

"That Kurt Riner has an alibi for one of the murders ascribed to the serial killer... That he might not *be* the serial killer after all."

Dubowski's expression didn't change, but there was a ripple along his jawline. "Yes, I've heard that rumor, myself." He swallowed, then went on, "If there was any real hope that my best friend isn't a multiple murderer, I would jump at it. As you can see, I'm not jumping."

Two men with a stretcher appeared and approached the dead woman. The sheriff and Jen took a few steps farther away. "Are *you* worried we collared the wrong man?" he asked her.

She took a long moment to consider it, then she sighed and shook her head. "No," she said stolidly.

"Then what is it?"

Jen threw a look toward the deck. "There's something wrong with that scene," she said in a low voice. "I don't know what it is, but something's...off."

The sheriff nodded slowly. He spent the next minute alternating his gaze between the pearly white landscape and the body disappearing into a black bag.

Finally he spoke. "The first death after the serial killer was always going to raise questions, rumor or no rumor. Even if it happened a year from now, people would still wonder—is he back?" He led Jen around the house. "I want you and Deputy Benno to go over this residence with a fine-tooth comb. Same with Ms. Brisbon's history. When I give my official report as to whether this was a natural death—or not—I want to be able to say it with *absolute certainty.*"

"You've got it, sir," Jen replied, though she would later wonder if her assigned task was more for her own benefit than for his.

* * *

Halloween! *That* was it!

Violet found herself in a room that screamed pretentiousness. A leather sofa, three armchairs, a majestic fireplace, fancy urns and vases, a hand-carved chess set, all quite expensive-looking…and all quite old. This room was preserved as it was for the sake of appearances; it looked barely lived in. One could do that, Violet supposed, in a house so large, but it seemed such a waste. She preferred to live as the Grogans did, making ample use of every room in their big house, without squandering their gifts on snobbery.

The room was promptly forgotten (so to speak) when Violet beheld the man sitting in the wheelchair. His voice, when he spoke, had been familiar, just as Ursula's had been, but she'd never seen Ursula from the front before. This man she *had* seen from the front—on Halloween. He and Ursula had been passengers on a Veil ghost tour. The man had walked with a cane then; that same cane leaned against the wall near his hand.

From beneath his silver-gray hair, the man's eyes bored into Violet. Despite having just insisted she come inside, he said nothing to her. No hostility, no words of welcome. He simply stared at her. Absentmindedness? Violet thought not. There was a shrewdness in his penetrating gaze that unnerved her.

Realizing that was perhaps his intention, Violet decided to behave as if he'd invited her to sit down, and suited action to thought. She stared back at him evenly. "You wanted to see me, Mr.—Lammwych?"

The man's mouth curled into an amused, greedy smile. "Call me Stan," he said in a friendly voice. "And I believe it was you who wanted to see us."

"Mr. Glass came to me today. He told me you're suing me for impersonating Roberta Lammwych, who I'm guessing is a—*was* a relative of yours."

"No relation."

This brought Violet up short. "No relation?"

"No relation whatsoever." He wriggled in his chair, clearly tickled at her confusion.

Violet set that aside for the moment. "Mr. Lammwych—Stan—I have never tried to impersonate Roberta—"

"Liar!" Ursula spat as she entered the room.

Stan held up a forbidding finger.

Grudgingly, she leaned against the wall with folded arms.

Violet tried again: "There was a woman, Delphine Burgess—maybe you've met her?"

Stan chuckled heartily. "Yes, I've met Delphine."

Violet took a deep breath. "She once got really excited about the idea that I might be Roberta, but she doesn't believe that anymore. And no one believed *her* when she suggested it. I never bothered to say it wasn't true because I didn't think it *needed* to be said. But I'm happy to say it now: *I'm not Roberta Lammwych.*" She looked from one to the other of them. When neither of them spoke, she continued, "I came here hoping I could convince you to drop the lawsuit. I can put it in writing if you'd like."

Stan's eyes twinkled, his mouth twitched. Violet sensed he was laughing at her on the inside. Whatever the joke was, Ursula was obviously not in on it. Her eyes squinted venomously in Violet's direction.

"Well, Ursula, what do you think?" Stan said mildly.

Ursula unfolded her arms. "You must think we're stupid. You say you're not impersonating her—when you've been doing just that since all the way back in October!"

"What?" Violet did a double take. "What are you talking about?"

Stan looked on smugly.

"We read the newspapers!" cried Ursula. "What, you think we don't get the news out here in Platte?"

"I don't know what you're talking about!"

"You're the Memory Girl!!" Ursula roared.

Violet threw her hands out, exasperated. "Yeah, I am! So what??"

Her response only seemed to make Ursula angrier. The older woman turned to Stan and pointed at Violet, as if telling on her.

Stan said to Violet, "Reportedly, Roberta Lammwych…had a perfect memory."

Violet was stunned.

"Oh, don't pretend you didn't know," snarled Ursula. "I've been on to you the whole time. First you pretend you have a perfect memory, then one day you miraculously remember who you are—Roberta Lammwych!"

"She…she'd be almost sixty!"

"If that Delphine person believed it, other people would believe it, too!"

Violet gave her a incredulous stare.

"You're a god damn grifter," Ursula went on, jabbing a finger at her. "Got everybody eating out of your hand. But your act doesn't fool us. If you wanted to stay in Veil, you shouldn't have come after what's ours."

"Our family's," Stan corrected her, a hint of warning in his voice.

"Yeah, that's what I said!"

Violet straightened. A light shone in her eyes. "So…if I had no chance of making a valid claim to Roberta's money…you'd have no reason to sue me. Right?"

Ursula eyed her uncertainly. "R-right."

"Do you mind if my, um, my lawyer joins us?"

Stan tilted his head. "Why?"

"Because I want to try an experiment, and I want her as a witness."

* * *

Fifteen minutes later, they were gathered in the same room, with the addition of Cy. She and Violet stood at the far side of the room while Stan sat before the small table with the chess board. For the last several minutes, he'd been arranging the chess pieces in a specific formation; now he was surveying the pieces beadily. Cy and Violet couldn't see the board's formation because an American flag was blocking their view. Ursula, who had dug up the flag from somewhere, held it like a curtain shielding the chess board. "Hurry up," she growled at Stan.

"I'm finished," said the old man.

"Well, then let's do it already!"

"No. We're waiting."

"For what?!"

Stan held up a cell phone. "I invited someone."

"Who??"

Stan glanced at Cy. "An *impartial* witness."

There was a knock at the door. Presently the thin young man—whose name, Violet had gathered, was Emmett—showed in the newcomer, a stout, middle-aged woman with curly dark hair.

"Oh no," groaned Cy.

It was the reporter, Kelly Upshaw. She didn't seem surprised to see Cy and Violet. Unlike Cy, she kept whatever displeasure she felt from showing.

"Impartial my ass!" Cy started to protest.

"No, Cy, it's okay," Violet quickly assured her. As a matter of fact, it was more than okay, it was perfect for what she had in mind—but she didn't say that out loud.

A pen and notepad materialized in Kelly's hand. "Miss Violet—"

"Still just 'Violet,'" Violet corrected her.

"How does it feel to be accused of fraud?"

"*No!*"

The sharp interjection made all three of them jump. Stan Lammwych's finger trembled at the end of his outstretched arm as he pointed at Kelly, but clearly it wasn't out of fear. "No questions. No interviewing."

Kelly frowned. "But in your text you said—"

"I lied," he said shortly. "I said what I said in order to get you here." At this, Kelly looked put out, but before she could reply, Stan plowed on, "If you're gonna whine and bitch about it, you can leave, and I'll find someone else. But you'll miss a very interesting story."

Kelly scoffed in disbelief. She glanced at the door, undecided.

Cy's eyes betrayed a glint of hopefulness. Seeing this, and likely knowing what Cy was hopeful for, seemed to make up Kelly's mind. She put away her notepad and remained.

"Violet," said Stan, "claims to be the long-lost Roberta Lammwych, who, once she's located, will inherit a six-figure fortune. As proof of this, she claims to have a perfect memory, as Roberta did—which is documented. She has requested we test her memory." Stan reached out and made one last adjustment to the pieces on the chess board, still hidden behind the curtain.

"Is that true?" Kelly asked Violet in an undertone.

"All except the first part," Violet answered.

"Come here," Stan barked. Violet strode up to him, stood before the curtain. "You'll only see it for half a second," Stan warned her.

Violet nodded. "I'm ready."

Stan gestured to Ursula, who threw Violet one last narrow-eyed look before quickly lowering the flag and then raising it back up.

Cy waited eagerly for Violet to rattle off the positions of every chess piece.

Violet took a breath. "Um…"

Everyone waited. "Well?" said Stan.

"Just give me a sec."

"It's mate in three," said Emmett tonelessly. Violet hadn't realized he was still there. She was impressed; he hadn't seen the board any longer than she had.

"Is that true?" Stan asked Violet.

"Um, I'm not sure."

"Violet," Cy hissed, stepping up next to her, "what are you doing??"

"Trust me," Violet whispered back.

Cy glanced at Kelly, whose notepad had reappeared and she was writing furiously.

"She doesn't remember!" crowed Ursula, pointing.

Violet made a show of deflating. "Shoot. You know what? You're right, my memory's not that great after all... Darn it."

"Violet, no!" Cy whispered in her ear, realizing what Violet was doing. "People in town will think—"

"I don't care what they think about me."

Besides Cy, the only person who could hear her was Kelly, who blinked.

"I knew you were full of it," Ursula jeered. "I'm gonna tell everyone you're a fake."

"Well," said Violet, "at least now you don't have to sue me or kick me out of town."

Ursula hesitated, then wrinkled her nose and waved her hand dismissively. "Whatever."

Violet allowed herself a small sigh of relief.

"You're lying."

The quiet words sent a chill up her spine.

With the exception of Emmett, everyone gave Stan a look of bemusement. Stan's eyes were fixed on Violet, who felt herself inwardly recoil.

Wobbily he rose to his feet, but his eyes remained steady. "You're lying," he repeated.

"Stan," said Ursula, "what—"

"Don't!" She had begun to lower the flag. He caught the end and held it so that it still blocked the chess board. To Violet he growled, "Describe the board."

Violet glanced apprehensively at Cy. "I...I don't—"

"Describe the board or I'll call the police and tell them you're trespassing."

"What the hell?" breathed Cy.

Even Kelly seemed troubled.

Violet was sure the sheriff's department would know such a report to be bogus, but there was little point in pretending anymore when her strategy had clearly failed. She drew breath, unsure of what she was about to say—

"Do it!!" Stan thundered. Violet flinched in fear.

"Hey!!" Cy stepped in front of her. "Leave her alone!"

"It, it's not mate in three," Violet stammered.

For the first time, Emmett's face made an expression. He frowned. "Yes, it is."

Violet shook her head, trying not to let the rest of her body shake. "The board isn't set up properly. The pieces, um…" She couldn't understand why she was losing it. She'd been through worse than this. The past few months, she'd fought and fled from multiple dangerous criminals. This was just a boisterous old man. How could he scare her so much? "The pieces," she said in a trembling voice, "started moving from the wrong sides. The whole game's invalid."

Stan's lips curled into a nasty smile.

"No!" Ursula shook her head vehemently. "She's peeking or—"

"Be quiet, Ursula," Stan ordered.

Ursula gawked at him. "What are you doing?!!"

"What *are* you doing?" agreed Cy.

With difficulty, Stan eased himself back into the chair, then he sighed. "You do have a perfect memory," he said, "which means we have no choice but to sue you."

The question *Why?* lingered on several sets of lips. At the moment, Violet couldn't care less why. She just wanted to get out of there.

Shrugging, Stan added, "Unless, of course, we find out what happened to Roberta all those years ago."

Then he ordered everyone to leave.

Emmett threw Violet a resentful glance on his way out, but she didn't notice. She was too dumbfounded. She was the last one out the door. She paused on the threshold and turned back to Stan Lammwych, huddled in his chair across the room. She felt tears running down her cheeks, but she managed to keep her voice even as she spoke:

"You could've just asked."

III

"I don't understand," said Cy. She and Violet had retreated to a booth in the Platte café. It resembled an old-style diner, except the menu had fewer fried items and more vegan ones. Before them, each had a steaming mug of hot chocolate made with oat milk.

Violet sipped, the warm, chocolatey sweetness bringing her calm and comfort, and explained, "I didn't get it either until just before Stan made us leave. All he had to do was let me pretend that I'd failed the test, and the issue would've been resolved."

"Right, so then why didn't he do that?"

"Because he doesn't *want* the issue resolved. He doesn't care about people thinking I'm Roberta Lammwych, that's all Ursula. But for some reason he wants to learn what *happened* to Roberta."

"Well, she's been missing for over forty years. I don't think he's going to find out."

"That's the point. He's heard of my reputation for...solving things, and now he's put me in a position where I *have* to solve the mystery of Roberta Lammwych."

Cy's jaw dropped. She was steaming more than the hot chocolate. "That rat bastard! How does he expect you to solve it when no one else has?! I mean, no offense, but that's like trying to find out who Jack the Ripper was!"

Violet stared pensively into her mug. "How exactly does the story go? About Roberta's disappearance."

Cy took a deep breath to quell her outrage. "From what I've heard at school, Roberta was sixteen, she was really depressed for some reason, and so, one day—"

"What reason?"

"Well, it depends on who's telling the story. Some people say she had a fight with her dad, others say a boy got her pregnant and then left her, one guy says she had an incurable disease..."

"Okay. What happened? What did she do?"

"One day she walked out her front door—she lived here in Platte—in fact it might've been that house we were just at—and she was wearing just her bathrobe. In winter. She walked down the road, wouldn't say a word to anybody. She went to the edge of the forest and walked right on in. And no one's seen her since."

Violet looked out the window. In as rural a place as Platte, the woods seemed to be everywhere. "Does anyone know where exactly she went into the woods?"

Cy paused mid-motion, with her mug half-tipped into her mouth. After a moment, she swallowed, set the mug down, and chuckled, shaking her head in mock disapproval. "You're gonna investigate her disappearance, aren't you."

"Until I can come up with a better idea. Plus, I'm...intrigued."

Cy downed the rest of her hot chocolate. "I don't know if it's really true, but there's a spot everyone *says* is where Roberta went into the woods. Wanna see?"

"Yes."

"All right." Cy got up from the booth. "Finish your chocolate.

I'll take care of the bill."

"No, I can get it—"

"Vi, relax, I've got it."

"No," a voice cut in. "I've got it."

Violet almost spilled the remainder of her hot chocolate.

Kelly Upshaw was standing by their booth.

* * *

"No!" Cy declared once they were all outside the cafe. "Absolutely—no."

Kelly eyed her bemusedly. "I haven't asked you for anything."

"You're about to! That's why you tried to bribe us just now. So whatever it is, no!"

"That wasn't a bribe, it was an olive branch."

"Why?" asked Violet. After what she'd just endured from Stan Lammwych, she had plenty of pent-up aggression to vent. "Why now, after hounding me for months? Back in November, you all but accused me of helping the serial killer."

Kelly looked away, inhaling deeply through her nose. She appeared to be gathering herself. Keeping a straight face, she looked at Violet and said, "Amy Chester was my niece."

Violet's anger crackled and fizzled out. Exchanging a glance with Cy, she said, "I'm sorry."

"No, *I'm* sorry. I wasn't myself that night, but that doesn't excuse my behavior. And obviously I was wrong about you faking your amnesia, so I'm sorry about that, too."

Cy waited a moment, then asked, "Is that *all* you're sorry for?"

"For now," Kelly replied evenly.

Cy did not look appeased.

"What is it you want?" asked Violet in a neutral tone.

"There's a story developing here. I want in. Whether the focus ends up being the Lammwyches' treatment of you or the unearthing of a forty-year-old secret of local fame, it's gonna be big. Either way, it's going to be your story. I figure, the best way I can make it up to you is to help you tell that story."

"What if we don't like how you tell it?" Cy asked acidly.

Kelly rolled her eyes. "I'll give you final approval. If one of you doesn't like it, it doesn't get printed."

There was a pause. Cy and Violet gave each other a long look, at the end of which Cy closed her eyes and sighed. Violet extended her hand to Kelly. "Deal."

Kelly shook. "All right…Violet, I recommend we go to the Veil Historical Museum. The guides love talking about Torrance Lammwych and his family. They'll have all the information we need to get started."

Violet raised an eyebrow. "Actually, I was planning to stop somewhere else first."

* * *

Are you sure you want to open this can of worms? signed Althea in ASL.

Yes, Violet signed back.

The eighty-something-year-old woman peered at her shrewdly through glasses that magnified her eyes to gargantuan proportions, showing off her sparkling blue irises. *Something serious must be going on.*

Violet nodded and gave her a tight-lipped smile.

"What did she say?" asked Kelly, seated next to Violet on a plush pink love seat.

"Nothing," murmured Violet. Cy, disinclined to spend time in Kelly's company, had gone ahead to the museum.

A sudden rattling announced Delphine's entrance from the kitchen. Violet had not quite ascertained the exact relationship between the two elderly ladies, other than that they shared a house and that they were not sisters. Delphine wheeled in a cart laden with more snacks and goodies than she could possibly have had time to prepare in the few minutes since her guests' arrival. Violet accepted a delicious blueberry muffin. Kelly declined refreshment.

"So," cooed Delphine, beaming as she settled herself into a rocking chair, "what do you want to know about Roberta's ghost?"

Before Violet had time to formulate her response, Kelly broke in. "Why did you believe that Violet was the reincarnation of Roberta's spirit?"

Repressing a sigh of annoyance, Violet translated for Althea.

Delphine gave a bashful chuckle. "Oh, I was just being silly. Though it would've been *something* if I'd been right, wouldn't it?" She, too, signed as she spoke.

"No one knew, at that point, about Violet's perfect memory," Kelly persisted, "so what made you connect the two of them?"

Delphine gave her a blank look. "I'm sorry, I don't know what you mean."

It was Violet's turn to cut in: "Kelly and I were just in Platte. We met the Lammwych family—"

"Oh! Did you see the spot where Roberta disappeared?" Delphine interrupted.

"We were going to, but we wanted to come talk to you before you started dinner."

"Oh, you're welcome to stay for dinner!"

"That's—very kind of you." They weren't making much progress.

Althea waved for their attention. As she signed, Violet translated for Kelly. *I think what Violet's trying to ask is* why *Roberta disappeared.*

"Well, no one knows! That's the point."

Yes, dear, Althea signed patiently, *but even if we don't know why Roberta never came* out *of those woods, there are events that can explain why she went* in. *That's what Violet wants to know.*

"And me," said Kelly.

Althea gave her a sweet smile.

"I see," Delphine said slowly. "Well, I'd say it all began with Torrance Lammwych."

"The lumber baron?" said Violet.

"That's right. If it weren't for his company, Veil might not exist today. He saved our town!"

Althea wrinkled her nose. *Well, sort of.*

"They asked me, not you," Delphine told her. "Anyway, toward the end of his life, Torrance became estranged from his only son. He was a millionaire, of course, but he was lonely. Most of his friends had passed away or left Veil to be near their children and grandchildren. In the end he decided to adopt children of his own. He chose a pair of teenage twins, Farley...and Roberta."

"She was adopted!" Violet leaned back in realization. "That explains it."

Explains what? asked Althea.

"Why Stan said that Roberta wasn't a relation." She turned back to Delphine. "So she and Farley took Lammwych as a last name?"

"Oh, yes. Torrance insisted. Over the course of the year they lived with him, the twins became quite popular in Veil. Or, at any rate, they were well-known, Roberta for her musical talents—despite her inability to read sheet music—and Farley for his, erm, reputation as a Casanova. Torrance became extremely fond of Roberta, but Farley, not so much. At first Farley pretended not to care that his sister was the obvious favorite. But over time, as she constantly got all the attention and all he got was disapproval, Farley grew jealous and resentful."

I'm not sure about that, Althea interrupted. *Farley was in my mathematics class. Whenever he mentioned his sister, he seemed amused, not envious.*

He was envious, Delphine insisted, forgetting to speak aloud. *It's the only way what happened next makes sense.*

Maybe.

You're getting senile in your old age.

You're older than I am.

Then respect your elders.

Althea stuck out her tongue. Violet repressed a snort.

"What are they saying?" whispered Kelly.

"Nothing, they're just sparring."

"Where was I?" said Delphine.

Violet resumed translating as Althea answered, *I think you should fast-forward to the night Roberta vanished.*

"Technically she didn't vanish till the morning after."

Whatever.

"One day, Torrance heard that Roberta had been seen with Johnson Thorne, an old, bitter rival of his."

"Wait a minute," cut in Violet. "Is that the same Johnson as in 'Johnson's Welder?'" Immediately she regretted asking, as a collective shudder passed between the two older women. Last Halloween, an intruder disguised as the infamous welder had broken into their home and terrorized them.

"Yes," said Delphine. "Torrance confronted Roberta, who denied it. Torrance was convinced she was lying. He thought Thorne had approached her and gotten her on his payroll to spy for him. Roberta tried to tell him she was loyal, that she

39

had the deepest gratitude for all that he'd done for her, but it was no use. The more she swore it, the more certain he became that she'd betrayed him."

"He disowned her?" asked Violet.

"No, but he said some cruel things to her."

He might have been planning to disown her, signed Althea, *but we'll never know for sure.*

Delphine nodded in agreement. "He never saw her again after that blow-up. She left the house in the small hours of the morning, wearing her best dress. The people she passed in the street saw how devastated she looked, but she wouldn't respond to any of them. She drifted along a dead-end street, pale and distraught, and when she reached the end, she just kept on going..."

Violet felt a chill on the back of her neck. She glanced behind her, but no one was there.

"I take it the woods were searched," said Kelly.

"Thoroughly. But there was no trace of her. Not a shred of clothing, nor a smear of blood. She was just—gone." Delphine couldn't help but glow with excitement.

"You said Roberta was wearing her best dress when she disappeared?" repeated Violet.

"Well, the one she gave her piano recitals in, at any rate."

"Not a bathrobe?"

"A bathrobe?" Delphine gave her a strange look. "No, it definitely wasn't a bathrobe."

Remembering what Cy had told her, Violet wondered about the discrepancy.

"Torrance drove himself crazy trying to find her, especially after he found out that his information had been false—Roberta had never spoken to Johnson Thorne. He wanted to beg her forgiveness. He posted a reward for anyone who could locate her, advertised in dozens of newspapers, promising to make it up to her if she came home."

"He thought she'd run away?" asked Kelly.

"At first. There wasn't any sign of foul play, but eventually, as all the investigators were stymied, he began to suspect that someone had engineered her disappearance."

Althea shook her head. *I still don't believe it. Farley wouldn't have done that to his twin sister.*

"He was *not* a nice boy."

Agreed. He mistreated the women he dated. But not his sister.

"He was fond of her?" asked Violet.

Althea hesitated. *He was her ally,* she signed. *She was his responsibility, and he was committed to it.*

"Did he have any idea what had happened to her?"

Althea looked at Delphine, who continued the story: "Torrance confronted Farley, accused him of planting the false information to turn him against Roberta. He claimed that Farley had set his sister up so he could kill her, spirit away her body, and make it seem as if she'd run away, all so that Farley could replace her as the favorite." She shook her head grimly. "He thought Farley would cower and plead innocence, or offer feeble excuses. Instead, Farley raged at him. In all the time he'd lived there, the boy had only ever been indifferent—aloof—when Torrance criticized him. That day, Farley screamed at him in a fury, smashed everything around him. He believed Roberta was dead—by suicide—and that Torrance had driven her to it. He shouted that Torrance had destroyed the only thing he'd ever loved."

Althea looked thoughtful but didn't offer any commentary.

"Torrance refused to believe him. He threatened to disown

Farley if the boy didn't confess then and there. Well, apparently Farley misheard him and thought he said, 'disinherit,' because he marched straight over to the desk, pulled out Torrance's last will and testament, ripped it to pieces and threw them in the fire. He spat in Torrance's face and told him he wanted nothing of his.

"That finally convinced Torrance that Roberta's disappearance was his own fault. Guilt-ridden, he went out for a drive…"

Kelly looked up from her notepad. "That was when he ran off the road? I thought he died in an accident."

Delphine shrugged. "It *might* have been an accident, but those who saw him last agreed he seemed suicidal. There's really no way to know."

Violet was frowning. "I'm confused," she said. "You said Farley tore up the will to disinherit himself. I'm assuming the will named both him and his sister as heirs. But people keep telling me that Roberta is due to inherit a fortune if she's ever found."

That's where it gets complicated, signed Althea. *First of all, there were three wills: one that left everything to Torrance's son, one that disinherited the son and spread out the inheritance among Torrance's distant relatives, and the last one, which Farley destroyed—or he thought he did.*

"He didn't destroy it?"

He destroyed the wrong will. He destroyed the second one, not the third.

"So when Torrance died, Farley inherited everything?"

Althea shook her head. *Not quite. Under the terms of the third will, Farley and Roberta got the bulk of the money, but the other relatives still received large sums. If one of the heirs were to die before Torrance, the other heirs' legacies would increase. However—*

III

"Farley changed his mind about his sister," Delphine jumped in. "He started to think maybe she *was* murdered—or perhaps even abducted. He tried to get people to start looking for her again, but everyone had given up."

He refused to accept his inheritance, and argued that no one else could inherit either—because it wasn't known whether Roberta was dead. His lawyers pled his case and it held up.

"So he was trying to force the relatives to find his sister," concluded Kelly.

If he was, then it didn't work.

"Aren't missing people usually declared dead after seven years?" asked Violet.

She was, answered Althea, *but Farley fixed it so that as long as Roberta's fate was unknown and unproven, no one could touch the money.*

"Is Farley still alive?"

"He died from pneumonia about fifteen years later," said Delphine.

Violet listened with half an ear as Kelly continued to ask questions, letting Delphine take over as translator. Inwardly she absorbed all that she had just learned, relieved to understand at last why she'd been coerced into this business. The Lammwych fortune was frozen in some account, unable to pass on to anyone for as long as Roberta's disappearance remained a mystery. If it turned out she was dead, then Stan, Ursula, and Emmett stood to inherit what would've been her inheritance. If it turned out that, somehow, she was alive, they might not get much, but at least they'd get *something*. Violet was, for them, the best chance that had come along in ages to answer their hopes and take the will's provisions out of limbo. In a way, she almost felt sorry for them. Almost.

43

Again, Violet felt a prickling on the back of her neck. She resisted the urge to look behind her. There was no one there. She was sure of it.

Almost.

IV

"What've you got?" asked the sheriff, leaning back in his office chair.

Across the desk, Jen looked at Deputy Benno, cuing him to start. "None of Sharon's neighbors are aware of any reason she might've had for ending her own life," he reported, "but then again, none of them knew her very well."

"Did she associate with anyone in Veil at all?"

"She had her groceries delivered to her every other week, early in the morning. Very often her lights were on well before sunup. The fact that her lights were *off* this morning is what prompted a neighbor to check on her."

The sheriff shifted his attention to Jen.

"I went over the house with a fine-tooth comb, as you directed," she said. "It wasn't too difficult; Ms. Brisbon was an orderly person. Not everything was clean, but it was all neatly arranged. There was no sign at all that anyone was in that house besides her."

"So you can say with certainty that no one came to the house?"

Jen hesitated. "I can say with certainty that no one came *into* the house, sir. But I can't be sure about the house's exterior. It might've been clear weather during the night, but in the early

45

morning, there were snow showers. Someone could've come up to a door or window and somehow enticed Ms. Brisbon outside, and any footprints they left would've been gone by the time the body was discovered."

"Did you find any evidence of this?"

"No, sir."

The sheriff leaned forward. "Did you figure out what it was about the back deck that bothered you?"

Jen slowly shook her head. "No."

The sheriff pursed his lips, then turned his attention back to Benno. "Who benefits from her death?"

Benno consulted his notes. "She made out a will to an Amethyst Brisbon. It doesn't specify how—or if—they're related. I'm still working on tracking her down."

Dubowski nodded slowly. "Did Ms. Brisbon leave behind anything worth killing for?"

"Not that I could find."

After a minute, the sheriff stood up. "I'm going to say something that doesn't go beyond these walls. If it weren't for circumstances being what they are—meaning Kurt—by now I would've closed the case file and called it an accidental death. What you've given me so far is not enough to keep it open."

Jen nodded her understanding, though she still looked troubled.

"Frankly I'm not worried about the cross-examination. Even if we say we're absolutely stone-cold certain, one person will always bring up the 'what if' question. For now, though, I want you to keep following these leads. Keep looking for possible motives. Re-check for physical evidence. Find Amethyst Brisbon." He looked at Jen. "If nothing else, keep digging until *you* feel satisfied you've covered all possible ground."

Jen let her fellow deputy exit the office first, then turned back to the sheriff as he resumed his seat. "Sir…"

"If you're about to ask if Kurt Riner has been released on bail—no. I've checked."

After a pause, Jen nodded. "Thanks, sir."

* * *

Violet pedaled up the long driveway to a house beside a vast field. Beyond the house was a barn. She leaned her bike against the fence bordering the field and scanned about for human life. She heard a hammering from just behind the house. That was probably the man Delphine and Althea had directed her to, but she decided to wait for Kelly and Cy before approaching him—

"Help me…"

Violet spun in a circle. For a moment she'd thought she'd heard someone's voice, as if someone were shouting to her from behind a thick pane of glass.

"Look at me… Please…"

Shivering, she zipped her zipper up higher. Before her sojourn to Antarctica, Cy's older sister had bought three matching jackets for herself and her family. They were color-coded by name: cyan for Cyanne, azure for Azura, and magenta for Jen. However, Jen's had proven to be too small, so Violet had ended up saving the jacket from disuse. She hugged herself inside Jen's jacket. Eventually the shivering stopped. The voice, if there was one, went away.

A voice from the real world made her turn. Cy appeared on her own bicycle. Her jacket today was not her cyan one but one that was yellow and hoodless, her favorite for biking.

"You all right?" Cy asked as she dismounted.

"Yeah," said Violet, not yet ready to share her disquieting sensations. "How are you?"

47

"Annoyed. Bethany Williams was working at the museum, and I had to agree to go to her sleepover tonight before I could get her to tell me anything about Roberta, and it seems like everything she told me was stuff you already found out from the old ladies. Bethany's probably going to try and 'cure' me of atheism—again."

"Then don't go."

Her friend sighed. "I've got to meet people in different circles so I can make more friends of my own. Or, to put it another way, I miss going out and doing stuff with people my age. No offense."

Violet squeezed her arm reassuringly. "Em and Neesha will come around. And if it makes you feel better, you're invited to dinner with me at Delphine and Althea's."

Cy made a face. "Wasn't Kelly invited, too?"

"She was, but I don't think she's going back. I got the sense that she was uncomfortable around the two of them." As Cy continued to look sour, Violet added, "At least she's finally taking us seriously."

"I still don't trust her. Ever since we first met her, I've had this feeling she's looking down on everyone, like it's her job to judge who's good enough for this town and who's not. I remember seeing it in her eyes when she first interviewed us, sitting all regal behind her desk, scribbling with her lizard-green pen. That's what she is—cold-blooded." She stopped as Kelly's car came into view.

As they watched her approach, Violet said out of the corner of her mouth, "It was a red pen, actually."

Cy frowned. "Are you sure?"

* * *

"Hal Clayton?"

48

A sturdy man in his late sixties turned from the shed he was building. Patches of white dotted his goatee and hair peeking out from beneath a wool cap. He laid down his tools and rose to greet the women. Despite the frigid weather, all he wore was a flannel shirt and jeans. "Who's asking?" he said good-naturedly.

Violet started to answer, but Kelly cut across her: "I'm Kelly Upshaw from the *Veil Chronicle*. My, um…" She glanced at Cy and Violet. "My fr— The three of us are investigating the circumstances surrounding the disappearance of Roberta Lammwych. We were referred to you by—"

"Wait, don't tell me," said Hal, holding up a hand and grinning. "It was Keith, wasn't it? Keith Dubowski."

"N-no, it was Delphine Burgess and Althea Sinclair."

"You know the sheriff?" asked Violet.

"Course I do. I was his second-in-command for a hundred years, give or take."

"Wait, you're that Hal?" blurted out Cy. "You were senior deputy before my mom?"

Hal took a step forward to get a better look at Cy. "You're Magenta's kid?" he asked with raised eyebrows.

"Uh, yeah." Cy wasn't used to hearing her mother called by her childhood name.

"My golly." Hal shook his head, amazed. Then he pointed at her. His hands were massive. "Under twenty-one?"

Cy glanced at Violet. "Y-yes?"

Hal nodded. "Just tea for you. Come on in." He waved for them to follow him inside.

Hal's passion was clearly craftsmanship. It was hard to tell where his workshop ended and his living space began. A half-finished rocking chair sat in the middle of the kitchen. Birdhouses on posts leaned against the walls. There was no TV.

Kelly, Cy, and Violet sat on stools beside the kitchen counter. Hal handed each of them a tall mug. Cy's was steaming; the others were room-temperature. "Would you like milk with that?" he asked Cy, who declined.

Whatever was in Violet's mug also looked like tea. She lifted it toward her lips.

"Careful," Hal told her and Kelly. "That's strong." He screwed the top back onto a tall thermos and set it against the wall.

Violet looked doubtfully at the mug's contents. She glanced at Kelly to see what her reaction was to drinking it, then saw that Kelly was doing the same to her.

"Now," said Hal, leaning against the stove, "I don't know what all I can tell you about Roberta. I wasn't around for all that. But I worked for Thorne's lumber company when I was in my teens—it was my first job—so I knew Torrance Lammwych when he was a young man."

"Then Torrance Lammwych worked for Johnson Thorne?" asked Violet.

Hal let out a bark of laughter. "Hell, no. You must be a newcomer to Veil if you don't know."

Violet gave a half-shrug.

"The company was owned by *Solomon* Thorne, Johnson's father. In theory, Johnson was vice president, but really it was only a title. Johnson never did any work if he could help it, so other people in the company had to take care of his responsibilities, though his father was too embarrassed to publicly fire him. Still, despite all that, Johnson expected the company to come to him once his father retired." He chuckled. "Got a nasty surprise when he found out it was going to someone else."

"Torrance Lammwych," guessed Cy.

"That's right. Torrance was smooth and slick and knew how to play the politics. By the time the company hired me, he'd already shot up through the ranks and was part of the management." Hal shook his head, a faraway look in his eyes. "Tor had a way about him that made everyone like him. Even the guys who got passed over for promotion never held it against him."

"Except Johnson Thorne?"

"Well…" Hal hesitated.

"I heard a theory that Torrance and Johnson started out as friends," remarked Violet, remembering a long-ago conversation. "And then they had a falling-out at some point."

Hal grinned as if at a private joke. "This is only my opinion… but I think that just might be true. Nowadays the general consensus is that Johnson played up to Torrance to try to get back in his daddy's good graces, or that Torrance tolerated Johnson because Solomon ordered him to. But I don't think so. I never knew either of them that well, I admit, but my impression was that they were real pals. Maybe Torrance wanted to help Johnson live up to his true potential. Maybe Johnson wanted to give Torrance a taste of life outside the workplace. After all, it was Johnson who introduced Torrance to Edie."

"Who's—" Cy started to ask, when suddenly Violet had a coughing fit.

Violet pushed the mug far away from her, feeling its contents still burning in her throat. "What is that?!" she rasped, pointing at it.

"Told you it was strong," Hal said with a grin. "I'll get you some water."

"But what is it?"

"My own recipe!"

As he poured water into a glass, Violet croaked, "That doesn't answer my question."

"Do you think Johnson Thorne bribed Roberta Lammwych to spy on Torrance?" asked Kelly.

Hal shrugged. "I told you, I wasn't really around for that whole part of it. At a guess, though, I'd say, probably not."

"Why not?"

"I assume you've heard of Johnson's Welder."

Kelly nodded impatiently. "The assassin Torrance hired to take out Johnson. The welder attacked him but ended up blowing himself up. Johnson survived but was a cripple for life."

Hal nodded grimly. "Never proven, but yeah, it was probably Torrance who hired him."

Violet's throat was still raw, so it was Cy who asked, "How did they go from 'pals' to sending hit men after each other?"

A barely audible sigh of frustration escaped Kelly's lips.

Hal pondered the question a moment before answering. "Whatever happened to their friendship didn't happen overnight. Whatever drama built up between them, they kept it private. Although…" He glanced at each of them in turn. "This is just my impression, but I think…I think it stemmed from fear on Torrance's part."

"Fear of Johnson Thorne?"

Hal shook his head firmly. "I don't mean a specific fear, I just mean—fear. You gotta understand, life is meant to have problems. It's meant to throw obstacles, tragedies, sucker-punches. Having a life that's perfect is just—wrong. We all know it deep down. But Torrance was so good at dealing with all the challenges, it was like they didn't exist for him. In short, he had everything...and slowly, gradually, he got paranoid he was going to lose it all.

"It started with his son. Torrance was so worried the kid was going to miss all the best opportunities—Bobby was *not* at all the smooth talker his dad was—that he started trying to run the kid's life. Eventually he drove him away. He began suspecting his employees of corporate espionage. In short, he grew more and more convinced that people were trying to take away what he had, to destroy his happiness. It was only a matter of time before he turned that suspicion on Johnson. Now, I don't know who fired the first shot, so to speak, but all of a sudden there were freak accidents happening left and right, close shaves and collateral damage. Torrance wanted Johnson out of Veil, Johnson wanted his place in the company back— not to mention his place in his father's heart, which Torrance had taken. Everyone knew it was open warfare between them, but no one could prove anything. We all just had to wait until one of them defeated the other. Eventually one of them did." He paused for breath. To Violet's disbelief, he took a long drag of the concoction he'd served her and smacked his lips appreciatively.

"Sounds to me like Johnson Thorne had a compelling motive to keep trying to hurt Lammwych," said Kelly. "Are you *sure* there was no connection between Thorne and Roberta?"

Hal half-smiled. "Well, let me put it this way. Back in the day, I was seeing this lady who was a nurse at the hospital. She tended to Thorne after the explosion. One night she told me Lammwych had come to Thorne's hospital room. She overheard him crowing, lording his victory over the man in the bed. Lammwych told him he would never see a penny of his family's legacy, and neither would any of Thorne's blood relations. It belonged to Lammwych's family now, and there was no one left who could take it away."

He paused, and Cy asked, "What did Thorne say?"

Hal shook his head slowly. "He didn't say anything. From what I heard, he hardly spoke the rest of his life. He was broken. Even if he did want revenge, he just didn't have it in him to scheme anymore, let alone recruit spies." Addressing Kelly directly, he said, "Turning Roberta against the man who adopted her would've required way more than Johnson Thorne had in him. I'd bet my life it didn't happen."

"Do you know where I could find a photograph of Roberta?" asked Violet.

Hal's eyebrows went up, then he lifted a finger and moved to a hand-carved bookcase across the room. He withdrew a leather-backed photo album and flipped to an early page, then laid it on the counter. "This was from a village fête—back when we still had those. Happened to catch Roberta and her father in the background."

Violet craned her neck to get a good look at the image. In the foreground, standing in what Violet recognized as Veil's central park square, were a young couple. The man could only be a much younger Hal Clayton; the beautiful woman on his arm might have been the nurse he had mentioned a minute ago. They were dressed in what was once called Sunday-best, as were the people on the platform behind them.

Violet was struck by the sight of Torrance Lammwych standing by the podium, looking through some index cards, evidently about to give a speech. He was handsome—even Violet, who was not attracted to men, could see that. Moreover, perhaps she was reading too much into one photograph, but in this candid shot, Lammwych appeared... The only word Violet could think of to describe it was *burdened*. This wasn't a proud man, satisfied with his accomplishments. This man, though he hid it behind a mask of decorum, was profoundly weary. From all she'd heard, Violet had begun to picture a man who was smug, even villainous. Now, in her mind, he began to cut a more tragic figure.

But where was Roberta? Hal had said—wait, there she was. Violet wasn't sure how she'd missed her; the girl was standing closer to the camera than her foster father. She was wearing a modest burgundy sundress. She was staring out across the park as if waiting for something, but not anxiously. Her face lacked expression. In fact, everything about her seemed unremarkable; no wonder Violet had missed her at first glance. This came as another surprise, as Violet had built up an image of Roberta as a center of intrigue and drama. Here, she seemed rather, well, boring.

Except for one thing. Violet squinted. Around Roberta's neck was a silver necklace in the shape of a key—no, Violet realized. It wasn't *shaped* like a key, it *was* a key, albeit a large one, with teeth and grooves. What, Violet wondered, did it open? Was Roberta wearing it when she disappeared?

Violet was completely focused on the necklace. She hadn't an inkling of the presence hovering above her, of the young woman shouting in her face, *"Please! I'm trapped! Help me! WHY CAN'T YOU HEAR ME??!!!"*

* * *

Jen's stomach growled. She knew she'd have to take a break soon; she could feel her hunger interfering with her concentration. It frustrated her that she'd made no progress with the case.

Perhaps that was because there was no progress to be had.

Maybe Sharon Brisbon's death really was a natural, albeit tragic, occurrence. Nothing in the investigation photos spread out in front of Jen indicated otherwise. The sight of an old-fashioned sewing kit in Sharon's living room had given Jen a momentary swell of anxiety; all those spools of thread lined up in rows— could that be an allusion to the song, "Pop Goes the Weasel," the serial killer's signature? *A penny for a spool of thread...* But then she'd remembered how clearly presented the past allusions had been. If the serial killer were involved, he'd have taken the time to remove one spool and place it where it was sure to be noticed—beside the body, for instance.

Anyway, why was she so worried about that? The serial killer had been caught! She'd helped take him down! True, she was concerned about the rumor that Kurt Riner might have an alibi for one of the murders. Though, to be honest, her misgivings had started even before that...

Jen heard a long sigh from one of the other work stations. Grimacing as she stood, she lumbered over to Benno's side. "You sound like I feel," she told him.

Benno rubbed his eyes and turned from the computer screen. "I have looked everywhere for Amethyst Brisbon. I have looked everywhere for any living relative of Sharon. I have looked everywhere for a single person who could be considered part of her life... *Nothing.* She was the epitome of solitude." He pointed at the mass of photos at Jen's station displaying Sharon's belongings. "If her death wasn't natural, it *had* to be for gain."

Jen shrugged. "If that's the case, whoever killed her must have taken something with them."

"But there's no record of her ever having enough wealth to possess something valuable! It makes no sense!"

Jen patted his shoulder. "I know."

Benno shook his head. "You know, I'm getting tired of being worried. We caught the guy who was killing people. We almost *died* catching him. We've earned the right to…to kick back or…or go out and have fun. Do you know, I've lived here a year, and I still don't have a life outside of work?"

A smile tugged at the corners of Jen's mouth. "Well, I think we could do something about that." She glanced at the clock. "We're both on overtime at this point. We can pick this up again in the morning. Let's go out."

Benno stared at her. "Go out?"

"Yeah, let's go to a bar, hang out, eat junk food, drink beers like cops do on TV."

Benno looked completely nonplussed. "I guess I never pictured you and me hanging out together. I mean, I'm the rookie and you're the senior deputy."

"I promise there's not a rule against it. Besides, you're not the only one whose social life needs a kick in the pants. Outside my family, the only person in Veil I've really hung out with is Myrna Redpath."

"What about Violet?"

This drew Jen up short. After a moment of thoughtful silence, she grunted reflectively. Then she said, "Help me clean up, then we'll go."

Benno winced as he stretched his legs, then went over to Jen's station and helped her gather up the photos to put them away. One photo caught his eye, and he paused. "Hm," he said. "Weird necklace."

"Yeah, I noticed that," said Jen.

"What's that supposed to be, a knife? A serrated blade?"

Jen took another look. "It's a key. A silver key."

V

Something warm, rough and damp rubbed against Violet's chin. Slowly she blinked herself awake. She found herself staring into a mottled, whiskery face with bright amber eyes. They were almost the same color as her own.

Violet scratched under the cat's chin, eliciting a contented warble. Roswell thumped his head against her collarbone, letting the rest of his body go limp against her. Stroking him, she leaned over slightly to see that her pen and papers had fallen off her lap and onto the floor by the sofa. The fire in the den fireplace crackled cozily. With Cy at Bethany's sleepover and Jen working late, the Grogan house was unusually quiet.

Violet's gaze drifted to the photograph of Roberta on the coffee table. Strange, Violet thought, that she should think of it as a photo of Roberta when the girl featured only in the background. Forty-two years had passed since she'd set foot in Veil, and Roberta was arguably one of the most well-known people here. Was she really that well-known *before* her vanishing act? Was the infamy surrounding her disappearance a result of her popularity? Or was it the other way around? Perhaps Roberta was a background character who had mistakenly been assigned a starring role. By all accounts, everyone at the time had assumed Roberta was deliberately targeted, whether through hubris, envy, or revenge, but what if it was none of those? What if her disappearance was a result of an entirely separate issue, and only connected with those others after the fact, out of a desire for answers?

Violet reviewed the image she'd formed from the varying accounts she'd heard, of Roberta drifting like a ghost toward the edge of town, disappearing into the woods like dust scattered in the wind. What the girl had been wearing might be in dispute, but all the stories agreed that she'd had a *look* on her face, a look signifying profound desolation and brokenhearted woe. The more Violet thought about this, the less it made sense. If Roberta really looked so downtrodden, why hadn't anyone approached her, asked her what was wrong? She was the daughter of the town hero, after all. Furthermore, if Roberta had gone out in the very early morning, how could anyone have seen her face clearly? Even now, when the days were gradually lengthening, sunlight didn't shine until well after what were considered breakfast hours.

From all that she'd heard today, really the one and only conclusion Violet could draw was that the last time Roberta had been seen was when she'd entered the woods. All the circumstances surrounding the event were guesses and theories, but that one moment in which Roberta had stepped out of civilization and into wild country had enough corroboration that Violet decided to believe it was true.

Violet still hadn't taken a look at the famous "spot" in Platte. She'd stop by there tomorrow after she—

A chill washed over her, starting between her shoulder blades and spreading down her back. She sighed through her teeth.

She was getting tired of this feeling. This time she would *not* look behind her. There was no one there. No one was watching her. There was no ghost haunting her. Roberta's spirit was not trying to tell her anything. There was no one in the house but herself and Roswell. Violet looked down at the cat as if for reassurance.

Roswell's eyes were fixed on a point above her right shoulder, as if at a person standing behind her.

Swallowing, trying not to let a change in her breathing give away her anxiety, Violet gently moved the cat aside, and turned.

A tiny spider hung from the lamp by an invisible thread. Roswell climbed onto the back of the sofa, across the table and sniffed at the spider, who tried to make a hasty escape. Violet let a breath of relief gush from her chest.

That was when she heard a loud BUMP from the kitchen.

She jumped up, her heart pounding…

"Ow."

Violet blinked. "Jen?"

Another bump followed. "Stop getting in my way!"

Violet hurried to the kitchen, where she found Jen trying to get up from the bench by the table. A glass and an almost-empty bottle of wine sat before her. Again, Jen tried to lift her leg and bashed her knee into the table. "You do that again and you're under arrest," she threatened, her words slurring.

"Jen—Jen, wait!" Violet came to her rescue, helping her extricate herself and then supporting her. "How long have you been home?"

Jen narrowed her eyes blearily. "How long have *you* been home?"

Jen was much taller than Violet and difficult for the smaller woman to support. Violet was afraid that if she sat Jen back down on the bench, Jen would consume more of the wine, adding to the problem. She brought her friend to the den, where Jen banged her shin on the coffee table before flopping onto the sofa, scattering more pages and sending Roswell scurrying away.

As Violet picked up the papers strewn on the floor, Jen asked lopsidedly, "You still working on your mystery?"

Violet wasn't sure how to act around Jen when she was drunk. "Yeah," she said. In an undertone she added, "That's what I thought you were doing."

Jen heard her. "Benno and I went for a drink. We went to the…to the bar with the…in the place…with the thing. You know."

"You didn't drive home drunk, did you?"

"Course not. I got drunk, and *then* I drove home. Wait…"

Violet forced a laugh. "Well, I'm glad you and Benno had a good time."

"Benno left early. Wasn't feeling well. Poor kid."

"Oh." Violet glanced at the clock. It was after one in the morning. "Well, then, what have you been doing?"

"What've *you* been doing?" All at once, Jen grabbed the papers out of her hand. On the top of the stack was the photo of Roberta, though it was turned over. Jen read the date inscribed on the back. She grunted. "That's the year I was born. Or the year before." She tossed the photo aside. "What's this list?"

Sighing, Violet sat down next to Jen. "It's a list of people who might be able to tell us more about Roberta Lammwych."

"But you don't need to make lists. You're a perfect memory."

At that, Violet almost laughed for real. "It's for Cy, so we can work out who'll talk to whom."

Jen looked more closely at the list. "These are all older people."

"I'm hoping to find someone who actually knew Roberta. Or her brother."

As Jen stared at the list, her expression grew peculiar.

"Jen? What's wrong?"

Jen murmured, "Older people…" She let the pages slip back to the floor, where they fanned. "It would have to be an older person…wouldn't it?"

"I don't understand."

Jen winced, rubbed her eyes, then shook her head. "Never mind. Don't worry about it."

Violet bent over to retrieve the papers again.

"I think the serial killer might still be out there."

Again the pages fell to the floor, but this time it was Violet who had dropped them. "W-we caught him, Jen."

"We caught *a* killer. But I don't know if he's *the* killer."

Violet thought back to the scene in the sheriff's office. "The person who died this morning—was that murder?"

Jen gave half a shrug. "All the evidence says no."

"Then what makes you think the killer's still out there?"

"Violet," Jen breathed.

"Yes?"

"I think she was one of his victims."

"Who was?"

Jen looked at her. "I just told you—Violet."

Finally Violet comprehended: the Violet that Jen was speaking of was not the one sitting next to her, but her childhood friend who had been murdered when Jen was eleven years old. The killer had never been caught. "Jen," she said gently, "you told me Kurt *pretended* he was the one who killed your friend. He did it to trick you."

Jen nodded slowly, her eyes out of focus. "He did trick me.

62

But I could feel it."

"Feel what?"

"The eyes. The killer's eyes, watching me, just like the day she died." Jen seized Violet's hand, startling her. "The killer's here, in Veil. Still here, after all these years. I know it."

"Um—"

"So it must be an older person! It was over thirty years ago. What sort of person is still committing murder after three decades?" She snatched up one of the fallen pages. "Hal Clayton—he's old enough. Maybe it's him. Or maybe Rod Piper, the radio anchor. Rabbi Metz? He's older than he looks."

"Jen—"

"Or what about those two old ladies who live together?"

"I really don't think it's Delphine or Althea."

"It could be anyone, Violet!" Jen turned to face her—and as their eyes met, she gave a little gasp. "Violet…"

Before Violet knew what was happening, Jen had her in a tight embrace. Bewildered, she returned the hug half-heartedly. She heard sniffling. Jen was crying. "Jen…?"

"I know we're really different—in age and everything—but I think you're one of the best friends I've ever had. I care about you so much, even though I never say it." She hugged her more tightly. "Please don't let anything happen to you."

She thinks I'm the other Violet, thought Violet.

But then Jen said, "I was so scared when you risked your life to save me that night. You're part of our family. I am so glad Cy met you. You make us better."

Violet was so touched, she didn't know what to say. She reached farther around and held Jen close, relaxing her head onto Jen's shoulder.

It was hard to tell, even for Violet, how long the hug lasted.

By the end, there were tears in her eyes, too. When Jen pulled away, her eyes drooped. "Think...I wanna sleep."

"I think that's a good idea." Violet helped Jen settle on the sofa and draped a blanket over her.

"Wait, wait," Jen mumbled, "I want to call my ex-husband, tell him he's a shithead."

"No, you can do that later."

"No, I'll be too sober later!"

"If you do it now, you might say it wrong."

"Oh, fine." Jen's body relaxed, her breath quieted, slowed to a steady rhythm.

Violet waited for Jen's eyes to close. "You can sleep," she told her, rubbing her back.

Jen whispered, "But he's still watching me. He never stopped." She turned her head slightly to look at Violet. "I can still feel his eyes on me. All the time. I pretend not to feel it, but I do. I can't make it go away."

The coincidence wasn't lost on Violet: she and Jen were both feeling watched. Though for Violet, the feeling had only been present for a day or two. Jen had endured this feeling since she was a child. Violet couldn't imagine what that must be like. Had she grown accustomed to it? On the surface, perhaps, but deep down evidently not. What could Violet say that might help? What would she want someone to tell her, given her own situation?

"Maybe the person watching you isn't Violet's killer. Maybe it's Violet, herself, watching over you."

Jen grunted. Then she closed her eyes.

Violet brushed some hair out of Jen's face, fondly stroked the back of her head. Then, with a sigh, she collected the papers and headed toward her own room.

"Violet?"

"Yeah?" Violet turned back. Jen's eyes were still closed.

"Is it bad that I just had a one-night stand?"

Violet nearly dropped the papers again. When she opened her mouth, at first no sound came out. "N-n-no! Not at all."

"Thanks." Jen dropped off back to sleep.

Perfect memory or no, it took Violet over a minute to remember what she had been about to do.

VI

"If this were a story, like a mystery story, then it would be so full of plot holes."

"What do you mean?"

"I mean, there's so much about Kurt's actions that doesn't make any sense."

Violet was beginning to like the Platte café's vegan menu. As she bit into her avocado sandwich, she reviewed the memory of her conversation with Cy shortly after they'd caught the serial killer. "It's like we've missed something," she'd said back in November.

"Yeah, maybe," Cy had replied. "Or maybe, now that the mystery's over, you're back to having nothing to do."

Is that what was happening now? Was she looking for something to investigate even after the problem had been solved? No, this is different, she told herself. Back then, she'd been afraid to let her guard down. The tension had lasted so long, she'd needed to re-learn how to live without it.

Jen, likewise, seemed to have gotten over her fears and apprehensions from last night. Violet had woken her up this morning to ensure she wouldn't be late for work.

* * *

"Here, sit down," said Violet, guiding Jen to a seat at the kitchen table.

"Can't," mumbled Jen sleepily, wincing again and again to get her eyes to focus. "I have to make breakfast."

"Already done," said Violet, setting a plate of scrambled eggs and toast before her, followed by a mug of coffee.

Jen stared at the plate, bemused. Then she looked up with some trepidation and asked, "What did I say last night? Wait," she added before Violet could reply. "Do I want to know?"

"W-well—"

"Never mind." She dug into the eggs with her fork. Just before eating, she said, "Thank you."

Violet smiled and began doing the dishes.

As she ate, Jen noticed Violet's papers beside her. "These are the people you think might know something about Roberta?" she asked, perhaps to establish that her memory of the night before wasn't completely blank.

"I hope so," said Violet. "They're all the people I've met in Veil who are the right age, though I don't know if they were all in Veil forty-two years ago. When Cy gets back from Bethany's sleepover, I'll go over the names with her."

Jen laid her finger on a name. "You should start with Peggy Allen. She's a retired lawyer. I don't know if she knew Roberta, but she was definitely living here at the time the girl disappeared."

"How do you know her?"

"I remember her from when I was little. She helped my father sort through things after my mother died. A couple times she even babysat for me."

Violet turned off the water. "I didn't know about your mom. I'm sorry."

"It's okay," Jen said through a mouthful.

Hesitantly Violet asked, "Your father's still alive, isn't he?"

Jen stopped chewing. "He and I haven't spoken in several years."

Violet gave a nod and turned back to the dishes.

"You can probably find Peggy in the phone book," said Jen, reaching over to rub Roswell's belly. He was stretched out across the table on his side, in blissful slumber.

The photo of Roberta wearing her key necklace lay on the table along with Violet's list of names. Jen might have seen it, except that Roswell was lying on top of it.

* * *

Violet had taken Jen's advice and called Peggy Allen, who was happy to meet with her. Her one caveat was that she had a very busy day planned, so if Violet wanted to speak to her soon, it would have to be immediately. Violet arrived at Peggy's address to find the woman just leaving by her front door. She was nearly eighty, taller than Violet but hunched over with age. Violet, bundled up for the frigid weather, was surprised to see the elderly woman wearing only a single layer: a sweatshirt, along with a headband and fluffy mittens.

"You're welcome to chat as long as you can keep up," she said to Violet, and proceeded to jog along the sidewalk. Violet had no trouble keeping pace with her, though Peggy's speed was faster than Violet would've expected for a near-octogenarian.

Speaking while jogging was slightly awkward, but Violet managed to explain her situation with the Lammwyches.

"I've never been an admirer of Stan Lammwych," Peggy re-marked with impressively little shortness of breath. "Misusing the law to coerce someone into helping him make a profit is very much in character for him."

"Did he live in Veil back then?" asked Violet. "I was under the impression he and Ursula didn't move to this area until after Torrance had died."

"Ursula was just a child at the time," said Peggy. "She's his niece, I think, or cousin. Anyway, she didn't come here until about ten years ago, as Stan's new caretaker, allegedly. But Stan was a Veil resident from birth." There was an undertone of disgust in her tone, and perhaps something more.

"Did you know him personally?"

"Only by reputation," Peggy said with just a hint of hesitation. "He rarely had a real job to speak of, but he was always trying to impress the ladies with shiny cars and other new toys."

"You think Torrance was secretly supporting him?"

Peggy paused at a street corner, waiting for some cars to pass before she crossed. Jogging in place, she said, "Torrance didn't like him enough to support him. That was no secret. But there was a, a suspicion about town that Torrance was secretly paying him to carry out illegal actions against his rival, Johnson Thorne."

As they crossed the street, Violet followed through on this idea. "So when Thorne was crippled and the rivalry ended, Torrance didn't have a reason to pay Stan anymore."

"I have no proof of anything I just said," stated Peggy, "but yes."

Instead, Torrance had bestowed his beneficence on Farley and Roberta. Stan couldn't have loved them much for that. A startling thought came to Violet: Could Stan have been responsible for Roberta's disappearance? But then why would he have sent Violet to discover the truth about what happened to her? Was it possible Violet had completely misread the motivation behind Stan's actions?

"How did Stan feel about Roberta and Farley?"

Peggy had just turned onto a short uphill slope. She waited until they reached the crest before she replied, "From what I heard, he was always very friendly to them. Whether it was genuine friendliness or a ploy borne of ulterior motives, well, your guess is as good as mine."

"What did you think when Roberta disappeared?"

They had come as far as the Catholic church a few blocks from Main Street. Evidently this was the midpoint of Peggy's route, as she sat on a bench in the churchyard to catch her breath. Violet sat next to her. "When that girl first vanished," said Peggy, "at the time I didn't think anything of it. I thought it must be some silly misunderstanding. Her stepfather had all but thrown her out of the house the night before, so wouldn't it make sense, I thought, for her to go stay with a friend? If I were her, I wouldn't want to go back to him, even if running away made everyone think I'd been kidnapped or worse." She sighed, exhaling a cloud of vapor. "Weeks went by and she still hadn't surfaced, and gradually I felt less and less sure she was fine. But it wasn't until the car crash that killed Torrance and his wife, and Roberta still hadn't come forward, that I realized I must be wrong. Roberta must be dead." She pointed toward an office building peeking over the tops of some evergreens in the distance. "I was working there when it happened, for Davis, Wells, and Davis. We were the firm that handled the Lammwych estate. That whole business with Farley and the wrong will being destroyed, and then not being able to carry out the terms of the will because Roberta's fate was unknown— a ridiculous set of circumstances." She gave a sad smile. "I remember Reuben Wells, my superior in the firm. He was the executor for the Lammwych estate. He died from food

70

poisoning not long after Torrance passed. His family was with him in his last moments, but I saw him briefly. I'll never forget his last words to me: 'Find Roberta.' He wanted me to find her so that we could fulfill our client's last wishes. Only we never did."

Peggy paused, and Violet jumped in with a question she'd been holding for some time now. "Did you say Torrance had a wife?"

"Yes, of course. Edie."

That was the name Hal Clayton mentioned. "And she died with him in the crash?"

"That's right."

No one else had even mentioned her to Violet before. "What was she like?"

Peggy considered. "She wasn't much one for being in the public eye, as Torrance was. She made token appearances with him when she needed to, but she didn't get involved in the community like he did."

"Do you have any idea what she was like in private?"

This time Peggy's hesitation was more pronounced. "I don't think she was involved in Roberta's disappearance," she said.

Violet said nothing but kept her eyes on Peggy.

Finally the older woman gave in. "In private she was a devoted mother. When Torrance and Bobby became estranged, it crushed her. I suspect she wanted to leave Torrance so she could be with her son, but for some reason she didn't—or couldn't. I overheard one conversation between her and her husband, which I probably shouldn't tell you about, but…" She shrugged. "It happened not too long before Roberta disappeared. They'd come to the firm to sign some business documents, but while they were waiting, I heard them arguing. Edie wanted Torrance to change his will such that his wealth would pass to his son. Even if they never spoke again, she said, he should still provide for Bobby's needs. She begged him over and over to leave his money to Bobby, and not to his more distant relations—in other words, Stan and Ursula."

"She wanted Torrance to disinherit Stan and Ursula in favor of Bobby?"

"That's right."

"Did she mention anyone besides them?"

"Well, Stan had a brother at the time, but he's dead now. I don't remember his name. I believe he had a son named Emmett. There were other Lammwyches, of course, but I can't remember them either."

Violet gazed across the churchyard, the wheels in her brain turning furiously.

Peggy sprang to her feet. "Still another three miles to go. You ready?"

But Violet didn't need to hear any more. She thanked Peggy Allen and remained on the bench, lost in thought.

* * *

"May I join you?"

Violet snapped out of her reverie to find Kelly Upshaw approaching her booth in the café. "Sure," she said distractedly, pushing aside her empty plate and drawing her chocolate milk closer. "What brings you here?"

"Just doing some legwork," Kelly said as she settled in across from Violet. "I was up part of the night trying to locate Roberta's birth parents, just in case her disappearance might have something to do with her life before she was adopted."

Violet nodded absently. "Maybe." She sipped her chocolate.

Kelly eyed her beadily. "You seem preoccupied."

Violet considered how much she might be willing to share with Kelly. Having worked together yesterday afternoon, the icy enmity between them had perhaps begun to thaw, but they were still ways away from mending fences. She directed her gaze out the window. Since her jog with Peggy Allen this morning, the wind had picked up. There was no precipitation, but the air was filled with swirling eddies of snow. Even in the daylight, it was quite eerie.

"You know," she said, "I've only been in Veil a few months, and I've helped solve several mysteries. But I have a feeling this one—the mystery of Roberta's disappearance—isn't going to be solved."

A frown flickered across Kelly's features, but her reporter's mien seemed to kick in, and her expression became neutral. "Why do you say that?"

Violet felt a familiar chill on the back of her neck. She reached back and rubbed at it. "Can I tell you something off the record?"

"Of course."

"Ever since yesterday morning, I've felt this...this presence watching me, following me. I know no one's behind me, but I keep looking back. Sometimes I even thought I heard..."

Kelly was evidently one who favored getting straight to the point. "You think Roberta Lammwych is haunting you? That her ghost wants you to solve the mystery of her disappearance?"

Her blunt candor made Violet laugh. "I don't know," she admitted. "In my heart, I don't think I'm someone who believes in ghosts. But if I did..." She crossed her arms ponderingly. "If I did, I'd say this ghost *doesn't* want me to solve her mystery. It feels like I'm being warned away from it. Like she's telling me there's nothing to find. Only danger." She shook her head. "I sound crazy."

"You sound like you don't really want to know what happened to her."

"But I do, though!" Violet spread her arms so fast she nearly knocked over her drink. "I didn't care yesterday, but the more I learned, the more intrigued I became. Now I'm dying to know! What could have happened to her?! Where did she go?!"

Kelly looked bemused. "Well…as a reporter, I'd tell you not to give up until you've learned everything you possibly can."

There was a challenge in Kelly's tone that stirred Violet's competitive spirit. "You know what? You're right. If I'm going to be a deputy someday, I can't let fear stop me from investigating a mystery." Her cell phone let out a *ding*. As she checked it, she went on, "Even if this case ends with nothing but a bunch of loose ends, I've still got to try."

Kelly looked more perplexed than ever. "There's also the fact that if you don't find out for sure whether Roberta is alive or dead, the Lammwyches will take you to court."

Violet put away her phone and started to slide out from the booth. "Cy's still stuck at Bethany's. I'm going to check something out." She slipped on her magenta jacket, then paused. "I don't have to go to court, actually. I've found out all I need to stop the Lammwyches from harassing me anymore."

Kelly's eyebrows went up. "Any chance you want to go back on the record?"

Violet gave a small grin. "A little while ago I called Henry Glass and asked him to arrange a meeting with the Lammwyches this evening."

"You're planning a showdown?"

Violet shook her head. "It's not a showdown if you've already won."

Kelly watched her curiously as she left the café.

Neither of them noticed a patron who was eavesdropping on them from another booth: Emmett Lammwych.

* * *

At last Violet stood before *the spot*. Just as she had felt when seeing an image of Roberta for the first time, the tree line at the end of the short, dead-end street seemed unremarkable. Violet pivoted to regard the gas station and the café on the opposite side of the street. Both were close enough that their occupants could've witnessed Roberta in the last moments of her known existence. Pivoting the other way, she faced the Lammwych house a few doors down. The house was at the head of a T-intersection. If Roberta had opened the front door and drifted outside out of hopelessness, her trajectory would've taken her along the front path and down the road straight ahead of her. What reason would she have had for turning this way?

Violet felt her curiosity burning like an itch. Why did she feel so driven to solve this mystery?

Because maybe if I find the missing pieces of Roberta's story, she thought, *finding the missing part of my own won't feel like such a lost cause.*

For a brief, mad moment Violet considered the possibility that she really was Roberta Lammwych, that something extraordinary had occurred once she'd stepped past the tree line and out of sight, transporting her through time to the present day, minus her memories. Perhaps Delphine had been right after all. *And she didn't even know about Roberta's perfect memory.*

She shook her head to herself, trying not to indulge the notion too far. Roberta had been sixteen when she disappeared, and medical professionals had confirmed Violet was in her early twenties. Not to mention, of course, the fact that they looked completely different. The photograph proved that.

But Delphine never said I actually was Roberta, a part of Violet persisted. *She said I was the reincarnation of her spirit.* And reincarnations didn't have to look like their former selves.

No. I'm not Roberta, Violet told herself firmly. *I'm standing on a spot where Roberta stood forty-two years ago, a few steps from the defining moment of her life, and I feel nothing—no familiarity, no dread, no foreboding. This place has no meaning for me.*

And then a peculiar thing happened.

Violet took a step forward.

It had not been a conscious decision. One moment she was standing, the next, she found herself moving. Perhaps the stubborn part of her wanted to see if repeating Roberta's last known actions would trigger any feelings. Violet might possibly gain some insight by retracing her footsteps. Still, it was a strange sensation: without any physical execution borne of will, one foot kept putting itself in front of the other, bringing the forest closer and closer. Violet wasn't sure if it was her curiosity that had taken over, or something else.

"No!!!" a voice somewhere shouted. *"Don't go in!! Don't do it!! Stop!! You don't know what's in there!!!"*

Violet couldn't hear the voice. Whatever was moving her forward, she surrendered to it.

A café waitress was just then refilling a customer's coffee. She glanced out the window, and what she saw nearly caused her to overfill the man's cup. Like everyone else in Platte, she'd been raised on the story of Roberta Lammwych. Every child had imagined the girl as she dissolved into the woods like salt in water. Now, as Violet neared the tree line, that familiar legend seemed to be coming to life.

Hal Clayton paused in the act of filling his truck with gas to watch Violet step from the paved road onto the curb.

Ursula Lammwych stared from her upstairs window as Violet passed between the first two trees.

Several people watched from multiple directions in shared fascination as an eddy of snow grew on the spot where Violet had just trodden, expanding into a brilliant, white whirlwind. Within moments, it vanished…and so had Violet.

Of course, she hadn't really vanished. She was only a few meters beyond the curb. But the ground sloped sharply down such that, with the trees grouped as they were, she was all but invisible to those in the town. It was quiet, peaceful. A stream trickled nearby.

Okay, if I'm Roberta, and I've just wandered listlessly into this forest, which direction would I go in next? Violet eyed the terrain critically. Of the few gaps between the trees that allowed for easy passage, none contained ground that would make walking easy. She tried one experimentally and nearly twisted her ankle. No, she couldn't imagine anyone hiking farther into the woods than this, not without a proper trail. If Roberta really had made it this far—for whatever reason—then, unless she had a specific route planned out, her next act would've been to turn around and head back home. So why hadn't she reappeared?

Violet turned around and began to head back.

An arm closed tightly round her throat and suffocated her.

VII

"Deputy Grogan?"

Jen stood behind Sharon Brisbon's house, staring at the deck chairs. She was sure, if she stared hard enough, she'd work out what was nagging at her. Of course, sooner or later, she'd have to process the events of last night. Upon arriving home, she had put off thinking about it by consuming a bottle of wine—something she hadn't done in more than two decades. Now she was using work to accomplish the same thing.

"Deputy Grogan?"

Jen replied without turning: "Benno, you don't have to be formal all the time."

"Yes, ma'am. Has anyone been here since we left yesterday?" He was standing just inside the sliding glass door, facing the interior.

"No one's supposed to be. Why?"

"I swear these items have been moved around. And the same thing over there."

Jen didn't answer. She was fixated on her own puzzle. The back part of her brain that registered what Benno had said started its own train of thought. Items had been moved around.

By the killer? But why come back now? Why not do it when they murdered Sharon? Except that no one had been inside the house, not the night of her death and probably not for a long time before—

"I've got it!" Jen exclaimed, making Benno jump. "Now I know what's wrong here!"

A voice from her radio cut her off. *"Grogan, come in."* It was the sheriff.

"Grogan here."

"I need you and Benno in Platte right away."

"Why, what's happened?"

"Violet's disappeared."

* * *

Violet snapped into consciousness and sat up with a sharp gasp. The quick movement made her so dizzy, her head dropped back and cracked against the concrete floor. She swore in agony.

How had she gotten here? Where *was* here? The last thing she remembered was someone attacking her, cutting off her airway until she passed out. Had she been kidnapped?

She lifted a hand to her face—and found a zip tie binding her wrists. *Yup. Kidnapped.*

When the throbbing in her head had subsided, she managed to sit up.

She was in a large, cluttered storage room, surrounded by hockey equipment and paraphernalia. There was one door and one window. The window was too small for a person to fit through, and the door would probably be locked. But first things first. Violet knee-crawled over to the nearest ice skate and began sawing away at the zip tie.

This abduction couldn't have been very well-planned, not

when the victim was placed within easy reach of a tool for cutting her bonds. It must have been decided on at the last moment. Something Violet had said or done had caused an act of desperation. Violet replayed her conversation with Kelly in the café. *"I don't have to go to court,"* she'd said. *"I've found out all I need to stop the Lammwyches from harassing me anymore."*

Suddenly Violet had a very good idea who her kidnapper was.

The zip tie broke with a snap. Her hands were free. She hurried to the door. Locked, as she'd expected. She dug into her pocket for her cell phone, but there was nothing there. Her kidnapper had taken it.

Reaching back and grabbing up the ice skate, she thrust the blade into the narrow crevice between the door and the doorframe. Whoever designed the door would've made it difficult to break in from outside, but from inside—she hoped— it should be easier to break out.

When the door popped open, she could hardly believe her luck.

Knowing the kidnapper might be lurking nearby, Violet looked around for a hockey stick to defend herself with. She quickly became vexed as the room apparently contained everything *except* hockey sticks.

Footsteps clacked somewhere beyond the door. Despite mounting panic, Violet struggled to think the situation through. If she fled from the room now, the kidnapper might chase her down. On the other hand, if she hid, with the door ajar, the kidnapper might mistakenly believe she'd already escaped. But where could she hide? The only option that looked promising was the pile of championship banners in the corner. Violet was small enough that the pile's added volume *just* might go unnoticed.

The footsteps sped up, getting closer. The kidnapper had seen that the door was open. Violet had no choice. She darted to the corner, pulled the banners away from the wall to make room for herself—

A vent! A square vent in the wall, just big enough for Violet to fit through. She pulled open the vent cover and slid inside feet-first. Once she was all the way inside, she reached out to close the vent cover.

The cover broke off in her hand.

The footsteps reached the door.

Violet seized a handful of the banners and yanked. The banners settled into a new mound that blocked the view of the vent in the instant before the door opened.

Violet kept absolutely still. Fortunately, the banners muffled the sound of her breath, but that meant Violet could barely hear anything happening in the storage room. After a minute or so, she thought she heard the kidnapper exit through the door. She remained in place another few minutes just to be safe.

She had another decision to make now. With the kidnapper gone and the door still open, she could make her escape. But it ran the same risk as before, especially since the kidnapper was no doubt combing the building for her (whatever building this was). Her other alternative was to venture farther into the ventilation system and try to find an exit that way.

Violet's instincts had told her not to retrace Roberta's footsteps. She'd ignored those instincts, and now she was here. Violet took a slow, deep breath and quieted her mind, listening to what her instincts were telling her now.

Uncomfortably reorienting herself—a feat she could not have managed if she were any larger—she proceeded farther into the vent.

* * *

Cyanne Grogan had to admit that, despite her continuous efforts to Christianize her houseguests, Bethany Williams was a good hostess. Cy had been planning to leave the sleepover first thing in the morning, but then her period started and she felt terribly sick. Bethany had taken great care of her, and now Cy was the only guest left in the apartment that Bethany shared with one roommate. She'd been lying on the sofa for hours and was finally beginning to feel better.

At the moment, Bethany was out giving another one of her guests a ride home. The longer Cy lay there, alone, the more bored she became. She considered getting up and riding her bicycle back home, but her insides pleaded for a few more minutes.

Cy had made a few new friends last night, as she'd hoped. The pity party she'd been throwing for herself since Em and Neesha had "dumped" her last month seemed to be drawing to a close. She still missed them, though. Better not to think of that.

She wondered what Luther was up to.

Her phone vibrated, signaling an incoming notification. Cy held up the phone and read it.

Period or no, she sat up straight.

The GHOST of Roberta Lammwych was just seen disappearing into the woods AGAIN—THE SAME SPOT AS BEFORE.

The notification had been sent by one of her classmates to everyone in the high school. It was accompanied by a slightly blurry photograph of the "ghost" entering the woods.

It was Violet.

Cy bolted off the sofa.

* * *

"She was taken." The sheriff pointed to a mass of broken twigs and trampled snow that to anyone else in the sheriff's department would've been indistinguishable from the rest of the forest.

"Are you sure?" asked Deputy Derrick.

"She was assaulted here and then dragged off this way." He followed the trail only he could see, Derrick in tow.

Jen was already on her radio. "Emergency! All deputies report to Platte. Abduction within the last hour. Victim is Violet Grogan."

She blinked. She hadn't added the last name voluntarily, it had been automatic. She hadn't even needed to add any surname at all—everyone in Veil knew who Violet was, and yet—

She decided it wasn't important right now. "Respond immediately!"

"I've got something!" shouted Deputy Benno.

Jen rushed over to find him holding a cell phone. "That's hers!"

The phone showed one missed call, just minutes ago, from Cy.

The two of them hurried to catch up with the sheriff. They heard him curse under his breath, and in a moment they understood why. The woods were bisected by a narrow road with fresh sets of tire tracks.

"Take photos," ordered the sheriff, "on the off chance we can match the tires."

"They've got chains wrapped around them," Derrick lamented. "That's going to make it harder."

"Grogan, where are you going?"

Jen turned; she'd run several meters uphill along the road. "To see where this leads."

"It leads to the old Harrison Farm, but—"

"Then let's go!"

"Jen, it's a dead end! That bridge has been out since the ice storm. The kidnapper didn't take Violet that way. They took her the other way, back into Platte. I'm sorry, but…she could be anywhere by now."

* * *

Lying on her side, Violet drew back her leg and smashed her boot into the vent cover. She felt it give just slightly under the force of her onslaught. Sunlight shone invitingly just outside. Violet kicked several more times, letting out a long holler. She'd been trying to keep quiet for fear that her abductor might hear her, but she was sick and tired of these *dark—cramped—smelly—vents!*

At last, her foot burst through. The vent cover went flying. A bit of wriggling and Violet was free. Ecstatically, she rolled about in the snow with her arms and legs extended, unwittingly making what appeared to be a drunk snow angel. Then, remembering she was still in danger, she got to her feet and stumbled away from the building. From the outside, it looked rundown. Still, there must be a driveway nearby. She circled the building, keeping her guard up.

Finally she found the front. Tall, broken windows looked out over a large parking lot. On the awning over the front doors, with a few letters missing, were the words: *P ATT IC R NK.*

The snow in the lot was unmarred but for one set of tire tracks. Someone had driven up, parked in front of the door, then left. That should mean the kidnapper was gone.

Violet sprinted across the lot toward the driveway.

* * *

84

Cy pedaled rigorously into Platte. She saw several patrol cars belonging to the sheriff's department parked up and down the main road, but there were no deputies around. She rode to the cafe and chained her bike in front. Then she ran toward the short, dead-end street where Violet had last been seen.

At almost the moment Cy rounded the corner of the café, Violet reappeared on the main road, out of breath, having cut through wooded areas once she'd spotted the buildings. She recognized Jen's patrol car parked up the street and dashed off in that direction.

Cy pulled her hood up; she was shivering. She had the awful feeling something terrible had happened to Violet. What had she been doing here? Had she found a clue to Roberta's disappearance? If Cy had just left Bethany's this morning like she was supposed to, she would've been with her...

Cy stepped off the pavement and into the forest.

* * *

"Jen!!"

Jen looked up from the truck with chained tires she was inspecting to see Violet barreling toward her. Jen caught her and held her tight. In her head, she said a prayer of thanks.

"Are you all right?" asked the sheriff.

After a moment, Violet pulled away and nodded to him.

"What happened?" asked Jen.

"Someone—knocked me out. I woke up in a storage room in an abandoned ice rink. I escaped through the vents."

"Did you see who took you?"

"No, but I think—"

"Sheriff!" Derrick bounded over, radio in hand. "Violet was just spotted! Someone at the cafe saw her going into—the woods..." Seeing Violet, he trailed off, bewildered.

It took them a moment to work it out. Jen and Violet looked at each other. *"Cy!!"*

* * *

Cy was gone. There were fresh signs of a struggle at the same spot where Violet had been taken, new tire tracks on the back road.

"It's like this spot is cursed," Benno commented.

"Maybe she was taken to the ice rink, too," suggested Violet.

Sheriff Dubowski shook his head grimly. "The kidnapper knows you escaped. They wouldn't have taken their next victim to the same place when you could just lead us to it."

Violet looked over at Jen, holding her cell phone to her ear. Her face was a stony mask of calm. As her call went to voicemail, mechanically Jen hung up and dialed again. She'd called Cy's phone at least ten times already, even though the phone had probably been thrown away by the kidnapper, just as Violet's had been.

Violet went into the café, where Deputy Derrick was interviewing the waitress.

"And then I heard screams coming from the woods," said the woman. "If I hadn't been taking out the trash just then, I never would've known anything had happened."

"Did you hear any other voices?" asked Derrick.

"No, just the girl."

"Why did you report that it was Violet?" He gestured at Violet.

"I was confused. Violet was here earlier today, and she rode a bicycle. I saw the other girl on a bicycle, and when she went to the same place, I assumed it was the same person. I did notice she had a different color jacket on, but I guess I just didn't think it through."

Violet drew a slow gasp. She looked down at her magenta

jacket. "Oh my god…" She strode over to the waitress. "What color was she wearing?"

"Excuse me?"

"What color was Cy's jacket?!"

"Uh, it was, uh, light blue."

Violet turned to Derrick. "I know where she is."

* * *

Cy opened her eyes and found herself in a dimly lit room, lying on her back, on the floor.

* * *

Both Jen and Violet jumped at the ringing of Jen's cell phone. They were sitting in the back of the sheriff's car, en route to the ice rink. Jen answered the phone like lighting. "Cy?!"

"Mom!" Cy's whisper was frantic. *"I need your help!"*

"Where are you?"

"I'm locked in a storage closet! I think I'm at the—" Her voice abruptly cut out.

"Cy?"

"That's the same place I was," Violet told the sheriff, "the ice rink storage room."

Dubowski got on his radio. "Attention deputies, Cyanne's location confirmed: Platte Ice Rink. Meet us there."

"Mom, someone's coming! I'm scared!"

"Give it to me." Violet held out her hand.

Jen looked at her. Violet's eyes held a promise. Jen gave her the phone.

"Cy, listen!"

"Violet??"

"Cy, listen to me! Go to the corner of the room!"

"What??"

"How close are we?" asked Jen.

In answer, Dubowski stomped on the accelerator. Jen and Violet were slammed into the backs of their seats.

"The corner of the room," Violet repeated, "where the banners are."

"How do you know about—"

"I'll explain later, just hurry!"

The sheriff turned sharply at a decrepit old sign pointing the way to the ice rink.

"They're coming in!" came Cy's terrified whisper.

"Cy, listen—behind the banners there's a vent. Get inside and then cover the vent with the banners. Then start crawling as fast as you can."

The phone was silent. They couldn't even hear Cy's breathing.

"Cy, are you in the vent?" Violet lowered her voice in case Cy was trying to hide. "Cy? Cy! Can you hear me? Cy!"

Jen looked ready to leap from the car and outrun it to the rink.

"Cy! Cy, can you hear me?"

"Violet!"

Jen and Violet heaved huge sighs of relief. "Are you in the vent?"

"Yes."

"Is she being followed?" asked Jen.

"Are they following you?"

"I don't think so."

"We're here!" The sheriff turned into the ice rink parking lot. Two more patrol cars followed.

"Pull up to the far left corner!" Violet told him. Then, into the phone, she said, "Okay, have you gotten to where the vent turns to the left?"

"Y-yeah. Violet, how do you—"

VII

"After another few feet, you'll come to a T-intersection. Go right."

"Derrick, Benno, and Hayden, get in there and detain anyone you find!" rumbled the sheriff into his radio.

The other patrol cars pulled up to the building's main entrance and the deputies rushed inside. The sheriff swerved into the corner of the lot, where he, Jen, and Violet alighted.

"Next," Violet said into the phone as she led the others around the building, "you're going to come to a spot where you can turn left or go straight. Go straight."

"Okay."

They came to the opening where Violet had escaped the vent. Jen immediately took off her jacket.

"Wait," said the sheriff, "you don't know how to get to her. You might get lost—"

"I can guide her," said Violet. "Let me use your radio and I'll talk her through it."

The sheriff eyed her doubtfully.

"Trust me!"

"I trust you," said Jen just before she dove into the vent.

A whimper came from Jen's phone. "Cy?" Violet heard panicked breathing. "Cy!"

"I can't do this!"

"Cy, listen to me. Pause and take a breath."

"It's too small! I can't move!"

"I'm at a juncture," came Jen's voice from the radio. *"Do I go left or straight?"*

The sheriff held the radio out to Violet. "Left," she directed. Then, into the phone, she said, "Cy—breathe and listen to me. You will get through this, I promise. I'm going to guide you."

"I want my mom!"

89

"She just went into the vents."

"Wh-what?"

"We're all outside—me, the sheriff, the deputies." She covered the phone a moment and leaned toward the radio. "Jen, go past the next two intersections, then turn right at the third." Back to the phone. "We're standing where the vent comes out, but Jen went in from this end to meet you. You're not alone, Cy."

"Okay." Cy sounded calmer.

Twenty minutes passed. Violet continuously alternated between the phone and the radio, gradually guiding mother and daughter toward each other.

Steady reports came over the radio from the deputies searching the ice rink. They couldn't find any trace of the kidnapper, though they did find an abandoned van parked in the woods nearby. Deputy Hayden was checking on its ownership.

"Violet," Jen said over the radio, *"I've hit a dead end."*

"What?" Violet looked into her memory. "No, it's not a dead end, it's a vertical drop."

"It goes down?"

"No, sorry, from your direction it goes up."

Some grunting. *"Okay. How far am I from Cy?"*

"Hang on. Cy, how are you doing?"

"There's a right turn with light way at the end."

"Don't go that way. That's not an exit, trust me."

"All right." She sounded strained.

"You're almost there, Cy!" Violet encouraged her. Into the radio she said, "Jen, she's close. At the top of the shaft, go ten feet, turn right, and..." She spoke into the phone. "And when you turn left at the next T, you should see your mom."

"I see her!" Cy cried in delight. *"Mom, I'm here!"*

Both Violet and the sheriff sagged against the wall in relief.

"She can see you, Grogan," the sheriff said into the radio.

"How can she see me? I'm still in the shaft!"

A shiver went down Violet's spine.

"Aagh, Mom, I'm not going anywhere. Quit shining the light in my face."

Dubowski's eyes widened as the same realization hit him.

"Cy," breathed Violet, "get out of there."

"What?"

"Get out of there!"

"But—Mom—"

"Your mother doesn't have a flashlight!!"

A shriek came over the line, followed by a jumble of noises, then a piercing scream.

"No!! Cy!!"

Silence…

"It's all right, I've got her," Jen said over the radio. *"We're all right."*

Violet nearly dropped the phone as she caught her breath.

"Can you see the third person?" asked the sheriff.

"No, they went down a side vent. Whoever they were, they're gone. Violet, if you wouldn't mind guiding us out?"

Another twenty minutes later, Violet and the sheriff helped Jen and Cy to their feet just outside the vent opening.

"Did you find the kidnapper?" Jen asked her superior.

The sheriff shook his head. "Unless he's still in the vents, he must've slipped by us. I bet he knows this place pretty well."

"How did you know the right route through the vents?" Cy asked Violet.

"What happened to you happened to Violet this morning," Jen told her.

"What?!"

Violet nodded. "I went into the vents and solved it like a maze."

"But—that must've taken you *hours!*"

Violet shrugged. "It was worth it. It let me get you back, didn't it?"

Cy gaped at her, melting. Wobbily she wrapped her arms around Violet and hugged her tight.

Jen laid her hand on Cy's shoulder. "Let's go home," she said with a sigh.

"No," said Violet, pulling away. There was a fire in her eyes. "We're going to the Lammwyches."

"Why?" said the sheriff. "What for?"

"For a showdown."

VIII

Violet was not one to crave attention. In fact, much of the time she was averse to it. On a few occasions during the months she'd spent in Veil, circumstances had necessitated her addressing a group of people, often confrontationally. It had required great bravery on her part.

This time there was no bravery. She was too angry to bother with it.

Anger from someone typically mild-mannered could be unnerving. Perhaps this was what quieted everyone gathered in the Lammwyches' living room—even Ursula, who still showed signs of champing at the bit. When the visitors had arrived minutes ago, she'd railed at Violet for impersonating Roberta *again* by disappearing into the woods the same way.

Ursula now stood in one corner with Stan and Emmett. Henry Glass hovered nearby, wearing his usual smug smirk. Kelly Upshaw sat in another corner, already scribbling away on a notepad; Violet had wanted the reporter here for this. Jen and Cy stood beside Violet, with the sheriff and the other deputies fanned out behind them. Hal Clayton was also present, standing amongst his former colleagues.

Sheriff Dubowski had just finished explaining what happened to Cy and Violet. He'd also mentioned that Hal had provided information as to the ownership of the van that was used in the abductions.

"Mr. Dubowski," began Mr. Glass.

"Sheriff," Hal and Derrick corrected him in unison.

"As you may or may not be aware, the Lammwyches rent out the use of their van to several individuals in Platte and Veil. These towns being so small, those individuals tend to coordinate with each other, passing off the van from one to another according to their own schedules. It's not unusual for my clients to go weeks at a time without seeing the van."

"You're saying it was stolen without their knowledge?"

Glass chuckled. "Why would I need to say that? You haven't offered the slightest shred of proof that the van was even involved in these alleged abductions."

Jen made a sharp forward movement. Violet caught her arm. She turned to Dubowski. "Sheriff, may I?"

After a moment, Dubowski stepped back, giving Violet the floor.

Glass looked even more amused than before.

Violet paused, but it wasn't out of hesitation. To her surprise, she realized she was enjoying this.

"I want to ask you something, Mr. Glass," she said.

"Unless there are formal charges being made, my clients are under no obligation to account for their whereabouts—"

"No, not them," Violet cut him off, "you. I want to ask *you* something."

This time Glass laughed out loud. "Are you accusing *me?*"

"Mr. Glass, just what are you getting out of enabling these people to harangue me?"

"Young lady, you can hurl your accusations all you like. It won't change the circum—"

"Did they promise you a share of the inheritance once it passes to them?"

Glass clearly wasn't used to being interrupted. His amusement quickly dissipated. "If all you're going to do is throw around baseless—"

"Because if that's the case, there's something you should know."

"And what's that?"

Violet looked past him into Stan's greedy eyes. *"There is no inheritance."*

A moment of stillness in the room, and then Stan Lammwych threw back his head in raucous laughter. Henry Glass did likewise, though it was slightly delayed. "I can assure you," he said in his most oily voice, "the Lammwych family fortune is quite intact—and vast."

"Yes, it is," agreed Violet. "I'm sorry, I misspoke. The money is there, of course, but none of it will ever belong to your clients, no matter what happens."

The grin started to fade from Stan's face.

Glass threw him a glance to show he was amused and not worried. "The fact that they're heirs of Torrance Lammwych would tend to indicate otherwise."

"Except that they're not mentioned is his will."

Glass sighed tiredly. "I assure you they are."

"Really? Have you seen the will, yourself?"

"I have reliable sources regarding the will's contents."

"Yeeeah," said Violet, deliberately drawing the word out, "so I actually had a chat this morning with a woman who used to work for Davis, Wells, and Davis, the firm that handled the Lammwych estate. From what she told me, it seems only one person actually laid eyes on the current will: Reuben Wells.

And he died not long after Torrance."

"You've clearly done your research, but what you don't know is that on his deathbed, Wells gave one last instruction—"

"'Find Roberta.'"

Glass was growing visibly annoyed. "Yes," he said shortly.

"Which everyone took to mean that Roberta had to be found in order to carry out the will's instructions."

"Exactly."

"Instructions that everyone assumed they already knew."

Glass sidestepped her and addressed the sheriff. "This is pointless!"

"I don't know," said Dubowski, "it's starting to sound like this will is worth taking a look at."

Stan locked eyes with Violet. Through his gaze, he leveled a warning at her, as clear as if he'd spoken aloud: *If you're trying to trick me...*

Violet held his gaze calmly. *No trick.*

Stan saw the truth of the situation, and to Violet's surprise he accepted it without protest. He lowered his eyes and sunk a little farther into his chair. Just like that, the conflict between them was over.

All this took place in a few seconds. "Fine," Glass was saying, "check the will. This is a bluff I'm more than happy to call."

"And what if I'm not bluffing?" asked Violet, turning back to him. "What if I'm right, and the will only names one heir?"

"Who?!" demanded Ursula.

Stan looked up with mild curiosity.

"Shortly before Roberta disappeared," said Violet, "Torrance had an argument with his wife, Edie. She wanted him to put his son back in his will, and to disinherit his other relations. Meaning you people."

96

Ursula took a step forward. "I see what she's doing! She's trying to say he made a fourth will! *She's a liar!*"

"No—"

"There were only three wills!"

"I know!" Violet shouted—another thing she was unaccustomed to. "I'm not saying there was a secret will. You're not listening." She took a deep breath and repeated, "Edie wanted Torrance to change his will in favor of his son, Bobby, instead of his other relatives."

Glass spread his hands. "And?"

Violet sighed. "Okay, one more time. Edie told him *to disinherit his other relations.*"

The response she got was blank silence—until Kelly said, "Are you saying Edie Lammwych tampered with the will?"

"No."

Benno and Derrick exchanged puzzled glances.

Violet scanned her audience. "Wow, really? Nobody's picking up on it?"

Jen frowned.

Violet looked at her hopefully.

Jen's expression suddenly cleared. "Roberta."

Violet nodded, smiling. "Exactly."

"What?" spat Glass, not following—and not happy about it.

"Oh!" gasped Cy. With an encouraging nod from Violet, she explained, "Edie told Torrance to disinherit his relatives *but not Farley or Roberta*—because she didn't need to!"

"Because Farley and Roberta were never mentioned in any will," Jen finished.

"Now you're just trying to confuse the issue," snapped the lawyer. "When Torrance made his third will, he—"

"You don't get it, do you," cried Violet. *"There is no third will.*

There never *was* a third will. The last will Torrance ever made was his second one, the one disinheriting his son in favor of your clients. When Farley destroyed it, he thought he was destroying a will that didn't actually exist. The last surviving will is Torrance's *original* will."

"But then why would Reuben Wells have said—"

"Mr. Clayton." Violet turned to Hal. "What was Bobby Lammwych's proper name?"

A smile tugged at Hal's mouth as he comprehended. "Robert."

Violet swiveled back to Glass and all but shouted, "*Find— Robert.*' Not 'Roberta.' *'Robert.'* He was giving instructions to find the heir."

Glass drew breath to argue more, but no words came out. The wind was gone from his sails. Ursula, too, was stunned into silence.

"Maybe now we can talk about all your whereabouts today," said the sheriff. "My guess is, one of you found out what the will really says, and was worried Violet was getting too close to the truth. You followed her…"

"Actually," said Violet, lifting a hand, "I don't think I was followed." She turned to Kelly Upshaw. "Kelly and I talked in the Platte café a few minutes before I was abducted. I think Cy and I were taken because of that conversation."

"Someone overheard you?" said Jen.

Violet nodded slowly, her gaze shifting back to the Lammwyches. "Someone heard me say that the Lammwyches weren't a threat to me anymore, that I didn't need to find out what happened to Roberta. That person is the kidnapper."

Emmett drew back slightly.

Jen came up beside Violet. She looked at the Lammwyches with tightly repressed fury. "Was it one of them?"

Emmett and Ursula twitched like cornered animals.

"No," said Violet, "it wasn't the Lammwyches."

Henry Glass took half a step toward the exit—and promptly found four deputies converging on him. "Hey—!"

"It wasn't Mr. Glass either," Violet said quickly.

There were several confused double takes.

Violet pivoted. "It was you."

She was looking at Hal. He opened his mouth in bewilderment.

She pivoted again.

"Kelly."

The pen froze in the reporter's hand. "Excuse me?"

Violet's breath caught for a moment. "You kidnapped me. And then you kidnapped Cy."

Kelly very deliberately laid down her pen and stood up.

Violet couldn't help but tremble. This person had choked her till she'd lost consciousness, could very well have killed her—even accidentally—and now Violet was confronting her.

She felt Jen's hand on her shoulder. The trembling subsided.

"Why would I do that?" Kelly asked evenly.

Violet threw up her hands in exasperation. "Because you *still* think I had something to do with your niece's murder. This whole time we've been working together, you've been hoping I'd let something slip. You pretended to offer an olive branch in order to get close to me. When I told you I wasn't worried about the lawsuit anymore, you were worried that chance would soon be over."

Kelly hadn't even broken a sweat. She gave no sign of nervousness whatsoever. "What exactly was I planning to do with you once I'd taken you?" she asked as if it were just another question in an interview.

"Honestly, I don't believe you'd thought that far ahead. You stole and used the Lammwyches' van so they'd be suspected, but other than that, I think it was your heart calling the shots, not your head. Maybe you were going to torture me, force a confession. I think it just drove you crazy that I was walking free."

For an instant, a vein pulsed in Kelly's forehead, then her perfect poker face returned. "A weak story," she said. "And what about Cy? Why would I kidnap her?"

"You didn't. Or at least you didn't mean to. You thought she was me."

Kelly barked out a laugh.

"That's why you didn't take her cell phone," Violet went on. "You thought you were kidnapping me a second time, and you'd already taken my phone. It's also why you took her to the ice rink and not a different spot. You didn't know I'd escaped through the vents; you thought I'd gotten out through the door, so when you put Cy in there, you barricaded it from outside. If you'd known I'd already gotten to safety, you never would've risked going back there. You were lucky the deputies didn't catch you."

Kelly said, deadpan, "I think I can tell the difference between you and Cyanne Grogan."

"Really?" Violet made a gesture toward Cy. "What color jacket is she wearing?"

At last Kelly's unruffled facade wavered. Shifting uncomfortably—and visibly trying not to—she answered, over-casually, "Blue."

"Okay," said Violet, "what about mine?"

Kelly looked at Violet's bright magenta jacket and said, swallowing, "It's violet."

Violet glanced at Cy. "You had your hood up when she took

you, didn't you? Other than the color, our jackets are identical." To Kelly she said, "When I first met you, you were writing with a red pen. Then you put it down and picked up a green pen. You're colorblind."

Cy looked from Violet's magenta jacket to her own cyan one. "Holy..."

Kelly's jaw trembled, her eyes fixed on Violet in hatred and fury. Any moment now she'd no doubt spew the familiar exclamations—no truth in it whatsoever, all supposition, no proof.

But it was a day for surprises.

In a low voice Kelly growled, "I don't think you were *involved* in my niece's murder. I think you *did* her murder." Her voice rose. "You're the real serial killer! It should be you rotting in jail, not the innocent man you framed!"

As she moved toward Violet, Benno and Derrick materialized on either side of her. In a moment Kelly was in handcuffs.

"Kelly Upshaw," said the sheriff, "you're under arrest for—"

"Why?!" burst out Violet. "I mean, sorry, Sheriff, for interrupting—but seriously, why?? What makes you so sure it was me? What did I do??"

Under restraint by the deputies Kelly leaned forward, bringing her face as close to Violet's as she could. *"I—know."*

Violet gave her a sideways look. "You know...what?"

"I know... We *both* know...*what really happened to Roberta Lammwych.* And we both know the connection—the *real* connection—between her...and you."

Violet stared, mesmerized.

Kelly flashed a vicious grin. "You're—"

"I KNEW IT!!" crowed Ursula. "I was right all along! She *is* a liar! I was right—"

"SHUT UP!!!" roared Kelly, making Ursula recoil as if slapped in the face. "You are NOTHING! Your niece wasn't murdered! I promised Amethyst I'd bring her justice! All you're after is *money!"*

A quick look passed between Jen and Benno. *Amethyst...*

Wriggling in the grip of the deputies, Kelly snarled at the Lammwyches and their lawyer, "If any of you goes after Violet again, you'll have to deal with *me. SHE'S MINE."* The deputies forced her out the door. *"Mine!!!"* she could still be heard shouting.

Shaken, Cy and Violet put their arms about each other's shoulders. "I was wrong about her," murmured Cy. "She's not too *cold*-blooded. She's the opposite."

Epilogue

"I'm ruling Sharon Brisbon's death as suicide," said Sheriff Dubowski with a tone of finality.

"Sir," said Jen, standing in his office doorway, "I really don't think you should close this case yet."

"I disagree. You and Deputy Benno were right. The 'Amethyst Brisbon' in Sharon's will was Amy Chester. Amy was Sharon's grand-niece; Brisbon was her middle name. It was Sharon's, too, as a matter of fact. She'd had it changed. That's why we couldn't find her relations before. Amy was likely the only person Sharon cared about, so when she died, Sharon lost the will to live."

"But I figured out what was bothering me," Jen protested. "It was the chairs out on the deck. Sharon Brisbon never had visitors. Everything in her home was arranged for one occupant."

"Grogan, cheap deck chairs around here often come in sets of four or five."

"But, sir, why would she have one deck chair turned toward another? All the others were facing the vista."

Patiently Dubowski said, "Grogan, the only person who could possibly benefit from her death was murdered two months ago. And I use the word 'benefit' loosely."

"Who inherits instead of Amy? Is it Sharon's next closest relation?"

"That would be Amy's aunt, Kelly Upshaw. And with all the rhetoric she's spouting about justice and righteous vengeance, I can't see her as someone who'd kill for material gain, can you?"

Jen shook her head, troubled. Everything he said made sense. And yet, deep down, part of her still screamed, pleaded for someone to listen, to believe, to help...

They're still out there—the person who killed my best friend. They've been watching me ever since, and they're still killing. Why won't anyone listen?

The sheriff laid his hands gently on her shoulders. "Jen, you've had a hell of a day. Go home, be with your daughters. Or, well, your—you know what I mean."

He was right, the girls needed her. Had it not been for that, she might have persisted. Jen went home, telling herself not to worry. The serial killer was behind bars. No one was watching her. Her family was safe.

* * *

Somewhere in Veil, there was a certain basement. In that basement, there was a photograph on the wall. A candid photograph of Sharon Brisbon.

Her murderer took a marker and drew a large red X over Sharon's image.

The killer thought about having lured Sharon outside that night. Thought about having turned one of the deck chairs to face her, to watch her terrified face as she slowly expired.

Sharon's was not the only photograph on the wall. It was one among dozens. Some had been taken within the last few years. Others were much older. All but a few of them had red Xs.

There was an X over the sneering face of Matt Foley.

An X over the smiling face of Marcy Temple.

An X over Marcy's father.

An X over Amy Chester.

There was even an X on a very old photograph...of Violet Hall.

And now an X over Sharon, who prior to today had been first in line among the few un-Xed photos. Not too far down the line was a photograph of three people: Jen Grogan and her daughters, Cy and Azura.

A low, giddy chuckle fluttered in the killer's throat.

Almost there.

* * *

"I know... We both know...what really happened to Roberta Lammwych. And we both know the connection—the real connection—between her...and you."

What had Kelly been talking about? What had she been about to say before Ursula interrupted her? Violet sighed and added those to the list of unanswered questions. The one and only reason she wasn't about to try and solve those mysteries right now was the guilt she felt: by indulging her curiosity and retracing Roberta's footsteps, she'd put Cy through a terrible ordeal. Roberta had waited forty-two years; she could wait a little longer.

Still, Kelly's parting shot had stirred an unsettling memory that insisted on replaying itself in Violet's brain. A memory of the serial killer telling her, through a distorted phone line, *"I wasn't lying when I said I'd been longing to speak to you. Ever since I first heard of you. You see...there is a connection between us."*

"What connection?" Violet had said.

"Oh, something very personal..."

Violet felt Roswell licking her hand, and she came back to herself. She was sitting on her bed in the clothes she'd just changed into. Cy and Jen were waiting for her downstairs.

Violet gathered up the cat and headed toward the door.

Staring over her shoulder, Roswell's attention seemed fixed on the ghostly figure following Violet, shouting at her with a voice that couldn't be heard. The same ghost that had been shadowing her since yesterday.

The ghost was a young woman with dark hair. Dark hair with a purple streak.

It was Violet.

"HELP MEEEEEEEeeeee..."

WINTER IN VEIL

A Mystery Novella Series
by Miles Ledoux

#1 VIOLET
#2 GOOD WITCH, BAD WITCH
#3 JOHNSON'S WELDER
#4 RING AROUND THE ROSIE
#5 POP GOES THE WEASEL
#6 APRIL
#7 OVERKILL
#8 THE THIRD WILL
#9 SALT & VINEGAR
#10 MEMORY LANE
#11 THE IMPOSTOR
#12 KISS ME QUICK
#13 BEHIND THE DARKNESS

Next time in Veil...

Violet approached the girl haltingly. She wanted nothing more than to throw her arms around her and hold her tight, as she'd dreamt of doing for months now. But was that what *she* wanted?

Violet was spared having to think of something to say as the girl gestured to her dress and stammered, "You look beautiful."

Since coming in out of the cold, Violet's cheeks had begun to lose their redness, but now they flushed anew. "I think I'm maybe slightly overdressed," she murmured bashfully.

All at once she felt a hand on her cheek. She looked up to see the girl's brown eyes staring into hers. "You look perfect," she said, her voice catching.

She still feels the same. Violet hoped that was true, as she could feel her restraint slipping away. Hungrily she reached up and grasped the back of the girl's neck. At the same time, she felt the girl's hand on her waist, pulling her close. Their lips met.

Violet cast away her mental control, letting her senses be bombarded. She felt everything times ten: the softness of the girl's hair, the warmth of her skin, the tickle of her tongue against hers, the press of her fingers through her dress. It was bliss as she'd never known.

But what brought her to tears with happiness was when she pulled back and looked again into the girl's eyes, and there saw the same longing she, herself, had been living with. As Violet's heart had left along with the girl, so, too, had a heart been left in Veil. Finally, she knew for certain, and it melted her.

Simultaneously they folded into each other, snuggling, each smiling into the other's shoulder. Violet lifted her mouth to the girl's ear and whispered, "Welcome back, Candy."

About the Author

Miles Ledoux was born in upstate New York and started writing murder mysteries at the age of nine. His first paid writing gig was in 2007, when a local theatre chose one of his plays for their summer melodrama. He received other royalties after moving to Los Angeles for graduate school, where he wrote, directed, and produced several mystery dessert theatre plays. He also started a side business designing and running mystery party games while working as a martial arts instructor.

Currently the author resides in Springfield, Vermont. Despite having lived in five different states, he has remained active in community theatre as a playwright, director, and actor. He also has a YouTube channel where he compares Agatha Christie adaptations to the books they were based on. His handle is @MysteryMiles.

Miles loves books, cats, music, Star Trek, Peanuts, and owns an ever-growing number of variations of the board game Clue. His favorite author is Lloyd Alexander.

You can connect with me on:

🌐 https://www.ledouxmysteries.com